THE FOUR BEAUTIES

Born in 1905, H. E. Bates was educated at Kettering Grammar School and worked as a journalist before publishing his first book, *The Two Sisters*, when he was twenty. In the next fifteen years he won a distinguished reputation for his stories about English country life. In 1941, as 'Flying Officer X', he wrote his two famous books of short stories – *The Greatest People in the World* and *How Sleep the Brave* – which were followed in 1944 by *Fair Stood the Wind for France*. These, and his subsequent novels of Burma, *The Purple Plain* and *The Jacaranda Tree*, and of India, *The Scarlet Sword*, stemming directly or indirectly from his war experience in the East, won him a new reputation and, apart from their success in Britain and America, have been translated into sixteen foreign languages. His writing took a new direction with the appearance in 1958 of *The Darling Buds of May*, the first of the Larkin family novels, which was followed by *A Breath of French Air*, *When the Green Woods Laugh*, and *Oh! To be in England* (1963). *A Lover's Flowers* (1971) is his most recent book.

D1048734

'H. E. Bates has always been interested in the study of varying stages of ripeness in women. Ripeness is all in the Bates' world – either just coming on, or *à point* as the French say of peaches, or beginning to be oozy-floozy. The title story here, about a cake-making teashop owner and her three daughters, all in turn dazzling the inexperienced young narrator, admirably displays his sureness of touch and the smooth voluptuousness of his flesh-colours. He is the Renoir of the typewriter' – *Punch*

'. . . Best by a long chalk is 'The Simple Life'. Written with a fine economy, it charts a woman's temporary emergence from gin-haze and self-pity in response to youth's innocent anxiety to please. From their first nervous awareness of one another until the pay-off which is very touching, the delicate cadences in the telling are just right' – *The Times*

H. E. BATES

The Four Beauties

PENGUIN BOOKS

Penguin Books Ltd, Harmondsworth, Middlesex, England
Penguin Books Australia Ltd, Ringwood, Victoria, Australia

—

First published by Michael Joseph Ltd 1968
Published in Penguin Books 1972

—

Copyright © Eversford Productions Ltd, 1968

—

Made and printed in Great Britain
by Hazell Watson & Viney Ltd
Aylesbury, Bucks
Set in Linotype Granjon

This book is sold subject to the condition
that it shall not, by way of trade or otherwise,
be lent, re-sold, hired out, or otherwise circulated
without the publisher's prior consent in any form of
binding or cover other than that in which it is
published and without a similar condition
including this condition being imposed
on the subsequent purchaser

Contents

The Simple Life

WINTER began in August: or so it always seemed to her.

Always, from the very first sight of it, she hated the cottage. She loathed the plain square red-brick box, its blue slate roof, the squalid confusion of currant bushes, black hen-coops, falling fences and apple trees in sprawling decay that passed for a garden, the muddy pond at the foot of it and the three withered willows sticking nakedly up from the water, like grey arms caught and fossiled in the act of drowning. Above all she hated the quiet clenching cold.

'Must get down to the cottage. Must go down for the weekend.' For two years and more she had listened to the same repeated cry. 'God, I don't know what I'd do without the cottage.'

She hated too the long Friday evening drive out of town, to what her husband fondly called the simple life. As the big motorway gave way to narrower country lanes and then to the flat almost treeless spaces of marshland and finally to a gated track across fields crossed by endless dykes feathered by brown reeds in which watching herons stood poised under a great width of empty sky, apparently fossiled too, she found herself increasingly imprisoned in a grey cage of impotent anger.

Perhaps above all she hated the voice of her husband, for ever reminding her of the joys that awaited them on arrival, at the little place in the country:

'The simplicity of it all – that's what gets me. That's the thing. No telephone, no television, no radio. No rat race. No appointments. Just you and the sky and, my God, the air.'

With certainty she knew, every Friday, as they came to the end of the field track and within sight of the cottage, what his first syllable, first gesture, would be:

'Ah! that air.' The fattish frame always seemed to broaden itself still further in the act of respiration. The immense exhaled sigh blew itself from his big loose mouth like a breath of sea wind. The well-manicured city-hands slapped his chest with a gusto not unlike that of an ape revelling in possession of its given square of territory. 'By God, you can fairly taste the sea in that air.'

The air, winter and summer, always seemed to her like ice. Always, from across the flat grey dykes, came the quiet clenching cold and always, five minutes after arriving, she started steadily drinking.

After the first reviving juniper lick of gin across her dry mouth she gave a great expanding sigh of her own. Often she didn't bother to take off her fur coat but merely wandered about in it, unpacking, powdering her face, smoking, staring out of the windows at the desolation of marshland, her drink never far away.

Her first immediate pleasure after the stimulating lick of gin was to draw the curtains and put on all the lights. The privacy of the world thus secured, together with the gin, made her for a time quite affable, even good humoured. The outer desolation she so hated was first shut out, then forgotten and finally replaced by a warm rosy glow in which she felt, at last, and for another hour or two, civilized.

Always, by ten o'clock or so, the last trace of affability, even civility, was dead. She began to be loose-lipped, strident, oily-eyed, hostile, bitter.

'I tell you once and for all, Mr Barty Bartholomew, this is the last time I come down to this rotten, stinking hole. This bloody fly trap. I've said it before and I won't say it again – I don't live in privies. I'm not used to buckets in the yard. You keep your lousy simple life – strangle it for me, will you, with love from Stella –'

Once, in a fit of gibbering fury, she let a burning cigarette fall from her lips and lodge in the collar of her fur coat, where it incredibly set up a fire which she allowed to burn for fully a minute before he realized the danger and started swiping it out with both hands.

'Oh! for Jesus' sake let me burn – I might just as well burn. I tell you, let me bloody well burn –'

In such scenes her face became an old grey-green mask covered by a sort of powdery mould. Her eyes, naturally green too, took on a dilation not only discoloured but both opaque and lost. It began to be impossible to tell how old she was. Her thirty-five years became forty-five, fifty, lost too between one arid meaningless decade and another. Her hair, tinted a new shade every week but varying not much from its own natural autumn to a fierier, fluffier squirrel red, became a mere dishevelled bundle, giving her the look of some spiritless moulting hen.

Somewhere beyond the drawn curtains, four or five miles away, was the sea. Some distance along the coast a new power station brooded like a windowless concrete castle. You could hear, from time to time, both day and night, the moaning bleat of fog-horns. These sometimes woke her in the night and she lay listening to them as if they were the echoes of something moaning inside herself, tearlessly.

All day, for the rest of every week-end, Bartholomew found his refuge in the simple life: chopping sticks, sawing wood, digging up strips of black marshland earth, pruning apple trees, occasionally fishing, sometimes merely walking, watching the gulls, the moorhens, the heron ghosts poised along the dykes. These unshared pleasures drove him too further and further into himself, into a bleak privacy of his own out of which, one crisp March day when he found her sprawled blind-eyed across the kitchen table, her mouth cut and bleeding from the broken glass on which she had fallen face first, he could only utter his own bleak impotent moan:

'I loved you once but what it was all in aid of – God, I wouldn't know.'

'Some rotten charity,' she said. 'Some rotten bloody charity.'

She woke at midday next day to an unexpected, astonishing sight: a deep late March snow. Thickly, a foot or more, it lay smooth on everything, a pure level crust, as much blue as white in the strong March sun, transforming garden, bushes, fossiled willows and the fields between the normally grey and desolate dykes with an amazingly tranquil and uplifting beauty.

With cold disbelief she stood and stared at it from the bedroom window. Already the hot March sun had begun to melt it on the southward side of the house. The roof was dripping like a running spring.

From outside she heard, presently, the sound of voices and then of scraping shovels. She looked down to see, below, on the garden path, a rosy and perspiring Bartholomew heartily shovelling snow and with him a dark-hared boy of seventeen or so, sweeping behind him with a birch broom. The boy was someone she had never seen before.

Wearing her fur coat over her nightgown against the cold she went downstairs. As she started to boil a kettle for coffee Bartholomew put his head round the kitchen door with cheerful explanations:

'It's Mrs Blackburn's son. Roger. His mother slipped down and busted a small bone in her foot. She sent him along to see if he could help at all. It's a hell of a snow.'

She said she was sorry about Mrs Blackburn, who came in twice at week-ends and once in the week to sweep up, scrub, wash up and light fires. It was very civil of her to be so thoughtful as to send the boy.

'Ah! coffee. Smells marvellous. It's what we could do with. The boy's been shovelling and sweeping since eight o'clock. He's strong as a horse.'

'I expect he could do with breakfast too. Ask him, will you? I'll cook him eggs or something.'

The reflected light of snow on her face, as yet without make-up, made it seem excessively pallid but at the same time tranquil. Her manner too had neither the brittle tension nor the morbid gloom that were habitually hers in the mornings. Snow seemed to have had on her a redeeming and calming effect of which she was totally unconscious. Even the offer to cook eggs at that impossible and sickening hour was something which failed to strike her as exceptional.

Bartholomew went out into the yard and came back to say yes, the boy would like breakfast. He himself would have some too: eggs, sausages, bacon, anything; the lot. It was heavy work out there. The snow was of the wet kind. They were both hellish hungry.

A quarter of an hour later the three of them were sitting at the kitchen table, the two men scooping ravenously at plates of fried breakfast, she with nothing but a cup of black coffee in her hands, her elbows crooked on the table.

The penetration of the boy's exceptionally bright blue eyes was the first thing that struck her about him. His forehead was massive for someone of his age, the dark eyelashes so thick and curled that they formed a sort of nest in which the eyes lay like two birds' eggs, brilliantly pure.

She found her gaze constantly drawn back to the eyes without consciously directing it. In return the boy offered only sudden sensitive glances of embarrassment, eating quickly.

'Let me cook you some more,' she said at last. 'It won't take a moment. There are more sausages. They have to be eaten.'

'No, thank you, Mrs Bartholomew. I really –'

'Oh! come on,' Bartholomew said. 'You need it. God, if we're going to clear the track as far as the garage –'

She went back to the stove. While fresh slices of bacon sizzled in the frying-pan with eggs and sausages she hovered over the table, pouring coffee, almost briskly. This exceptional behaviour for one who normally went about at that hour of the day in a kind of sour post-alcoholic lethargy so astonished Bartholomew that he was actually moved to make jokes about it.

'We're very chipper this morning, aren't we? Bright as a skylark.'

Was she? she said. She hadn't noticed it. She supposed it was the snow.

The word skylark suddenly caused the boy to stop eating. Shyly he said that in fact skylarks were singing already. He'd heard one only yesterday.

'I thought skylarks only sang in summer,' she said.

'Oh! no, they're beginning now.'

'What do they look like?' she said, 'I've never seen one.'

Sheer disbelief at this confession of hers kept him, for some moments, from giving any answer. Then he said that he wouldn't be surprised if they even sang today, in the snow. The sun was warm enough.

'I should have thought the poor things would get frozen to death.'

Oh! no, he said. It was quite likely they might hear one. If they did he'd point it out to her.

'That would be marvellous,' she said.

Bartholomew laughed. 'We'll be having you take up ornithology any moment now,' he said, 'under Roger's tuition. Eh, Roger?'

'You don't see many birds here,' she said.

Oh! there she was wrong, the boy said. The marsh was full of birds. All kinds of birds. Waders, sea-birds, herons, kingfishers, even wild geese sometimes.

She laughed too. She had to confess she'd never seen anything but a sparrow all the time they'd lived in the house. But then she'd no doubt that his eyes were keener than hers.

Bartholomew, drinking the last of his coffee and getting up from the table, seized the moment as an opportunity for another joke.

'Well, we must be off. Any more for the Skylark –?'

'Roger hasn't finished his breakfast yet. Don't rush the boy.'

'Can't wait. Must off. I'll start in by the garage.'

For some ten minutes more she remained alone with the boy, she with her back to the window, he facing her. The continued fascination wrought by the brilliant birds' egg eyes actually started to make her unsure of herself. She started to light a cigarette, fingers trembling as they so often did in the morning, and promptly dropped the box of matches on the kitchen floor.

The boy got up from the table and rushed to pick it up. The cigarette trembled in her lips and in a sudden impulse he struck a match and lit it for her.

'Thank you, Roger. That's very sweet of you.'

He went back to his plate quickly, without a word.

'Does your mother have to go to hospital?'

He said he thought for X-ray. Tomorrow.

'Do tell her how sorry I am. She won't be able to work for some time?'

No, but that was all right. She needn't worry about that. He would come in instead.

'Yes? You mean for scrubbing and washing up and all that?'

Oh ! yes, he could do all those things. Cooking too. And even, if she wanted, he could wait at table. He'd done it several times for Colonel Blakeney, when he had big parties and things.

'Well, that's nice to know.'

He at last finished his breakfast and went outside, saying as he did so that he would call her if and when he heard the skylark.

'Do I need boots out there?' she said.

Oh ! no, he said, the path was clear. In fact it was drying already in the sun.

Suddenly she felt impelled to go upstairs and dress. Normally she slouched about all morning half-dressed, in a smoky dream. Now she found herself putting on a green tweed costume, brushing and spraying her hair, making up and even, at the very last moment, putting on a pair of small pearl ear-rings and a single row of pearls.

In doing so she forgot the dirty dishes left from breakfast. Facing them with the realisation that she had done something stupid she felt a spasm of self-vexation, followed by a sudden craving for the first drink of the day. She had already started to pour out a half tumbler of gin when she heard the boy's voice call from the yard :

'Mrs Bartholomew !'

She went outside. The strong clear March sun was already hot. Snow was melting and dripping everywhere. The power and brilliance of the sun had also a curious effect of magnification. Framed against snow and the clearest of clear blue skies the boy seemed to be altogether taller, bigger in frame, than when sitting at the breakfast table. Snow light also heightened remarkably the remorseless young brilliance of the eyes.

He raised a hand to the sky. 'Up there. Straight overhead. See him?'

She lifted her face, eyes dazzled.

'Can't see a thing.'

'Straight up. You can hear him anyway, can't you?'

She stood for some moments staring and listening, eyes dazzled by sun, neither seeing nor hearing a thing. Then she finally managed to tune her ears to the thin trembling of lark song, cascading down, as it were, from a great vacuum.

'Oh! I hear it now. Marvellous. But I still can't see a thing.'

He dropped his snow shovel on the path, walked down the path to join her and pointed to the sky.

'You're not looking in the right direction.' He stood close by her, holding her right arm just below the elbow. 'No, not that way. Overhead. More overhead.'

She stared into the sky with eyes screwed up, again seeing nothing.

'I said your eyes were keener than mine.'

'It's farther up than you're looking, Mrs Bartholomew. Look farther up.'

She laughed. 'I'm looking a million miles up now.'

'Perhaps you're looking too much against the sun.'

'I'm just plain stupid, that's what.'

Suddenly she gave a cry. In a moment of unexpected revelation both sound and sight of the lark, from a height that seemed to her impossibly distant, merged together. She became conscious of a moment of great, simple, exquisite pleasure and in the unremitting thrill of it she actually threw up both hands.

'It's the most beautiful thing in the world,' she said, 'it's the most beautiful sound I ever heard.'

This moment of snow and skylark crystallized itself in her mind in imperishable fashion. For the first time she found herself actually extracting pleasure from the cottage, the isolation, the marsh and the entire simplicity of it all.

'Roger tells me he can do things. Chores and so on. Cooking. He paints and hangs wall-paper and does gardening and all that. He can even wait at table.'

'Don't tell me we're about to give grand dinner parties

with butlers and caviare. We've got this place for escape –'

'I'm not talking about that. I just thought I'd ask him to paint and paper the kitchen. It's never been done. The window frames have got cracks you could put a mouse through. I thought something simple and clean – just plain red and white. To make it brighter.'

'Far be it from me to do anything to come between you and the house.'

'I'd like to do it.'

'Good. You'll be telling me next you've cooked up some affection for the place.'

Some time later she appeared to change her mind about this. She was uneasy, she said, about leaving the boy alone in the house. You never knew quite with these people. You didn't know whether to trust them with the key.

'You trust Mrs Blackburn.'

She knew that, but somehow –

'Solution's easy. Stay down here for the week. You can then superintend. Keep the watchful eye.'

She agreed, after some hesitation, that this was a likely solution. But she would need the car. She would have to drive into Seahaven to get paint and things. Not that she was all that fond of driving in snow.

'The snow will have gone by tomorrow. They're forecasting rain.'

She said she hoped the snow would stay for a time. She really loved the snow.

The next day the boy prepared to decorate the kitchen. Snow still covered the landscape outside except for occasional dark islands melted by sun. The strong reflected light of it showed up unmercifully every shabby crack, every smoky shadow, in the cramped brick-floored room and she said:

'You feel you want to push the walls out six feet or so. You think red's too strong?'

The boy said he thought green would be better. Red was too strong, too fussy.

'I believe you've got taste,' she said.

Wearing a pair of old chamois gloves she spent the greater part of the first day rubbing down the old paint with sandpaper while the boy, wearing a thick tattered blue sweater with a heavy rolled collar, filled the many cracks in the walls with new plaster.

'There's a strange smell of fish about the place,' she said once.

He at once flushed sharply and apologized. He was afraid it was his old sweater she could smell. It was the one he went sea-fishing in.

'Oh! you go fishing? You don't mean you actually catch things?'

Oh! yes, he went almost every night. He mostly caught small cod and plaice and occasionally soles.

She marvelled. 'You clever thing. You fish from a boat?'

No, he said, from the shore. He wasn't always lucky, of course, but seven or eight times out of ten he caught something or other. Did she like fish? He'd bring her something, a sole perhaps, next time he had any luck.

'That's terribly sweet of you. Yes, I adore fish. I suppose you never get lobster?'

No, he never got lobster. But he knew a boatman who often did. She had only to ask and he would get her lobster any day.

'You marvellous man.'

These casual utterances of hers, apparently effusive but in reality nothing of the kind, had on him the disturbing effect of pure open flattery. It was only natural that, as the day went on, he began to feel that he had aroused in her something like affection. Sensitively anxious to do nothing to offend her in any way he also threw off the sweater, with its slightly rank odour of fish, and worked in his shirt sleeves, revealing dark muscular arms sun-brown to the elbows.

At intervals she made tea for him and poured a drink for herself. 'I'll get some beer in tomorrow for you if you'd prefer it instead of tea.'

No, he was all right with tea. He was a great tea man.

Sometimes in these conversations she found herself caught up again, unwittingly trapped, by the intense vividness of the strong blue eyes, disturbingly limpid under the equally strong black brows. Once or twice he looked at her in the same precise moment, his gaze caught and held by hers, uneasily.

By the end of the afternoon she confessed to being tired, in fact absolutely worn out. 'Aren't you tired? You've worked like a black.'

No, he wasn't tired. He never got tired.

'Ah! but you're young,' she said. 'You're young.'

The next morning he arrived with a basket of fish, two fair-sized plaice, a sole and a small cod. Again she marvelled. He'd fished, he told her, until two in the morning. He didn't get his first bite until almost one o'clock.

'Oh! you poor lamb. You must have been frozen.'

Hadn't noticed it, he said, and again she marvelled.

'What am I going to do with all this fish?' she said once. 'It's enough to keep me going for weeks. I hardly eat a thing.'

He would, he said, cook it for her if she liked. He loved to cook. The sole would be better kept a day or two but the plaice were better fresh. He'd be glad to cook them for lunch for her.

'It's awfully sweet of you but I don't think I could eat fish with the kitchen in this mess.'

Let him cook them for dinner then, he said.

'Oh! would you? That would be marvellously nice of you. But even then I couldn't manage the half of it. You'd have to eat too and help me out.'

By seven o'clock that evening he was grilling the two plaice for her and preparing to fry four cod steaks for himself. He had put on a sort of white mess jacket in which to do the cooking and it gave him a correct, professional air. He had also cooked potatoes, made a salad and *sauce tartare*.

'I marvel at the way you do things,' she said. 'You're so calm. You never get flustered. Me, I should go crazy doing all this. As it is I sit here not doing a damn thing. Not even opening the wine.'

He had, he said, already opened the wine.

'I thought we ought to have wine,' she said. 'I hope it's all right. The *Chablis* was the only decent one I could find.'

They ate eventually in the sitting-room, by the light of a pair of candles, in a golden glow. She never tired of saying how terribly marvellous the plaice was. She had never eaten such plaice. You could fairly taste the sea in it. And the sauce. It was a dream of a sauce. He was a genius. She would like to employ him for ever.

'I'll cook for you any time,' he said, 'whenever you say.'

'You dear boy.'

Such casual, effusive terms came to her naturally. She never dreamed that they might be interpreted by him as expressions of affection. Just as naturally she sometimes called him darling.

After the meal he insisted on washing up the dishes while she sat curled up on the hearth, in front of a wood fire, sipping brandy. When he had finished at the kitchen sink she was insistent that he sit by the fire too. By this time she had slipped on a short olive green house-coat and the colour of it heightened appreciably, in the firelight, the deep autumn copper of her thick crown of hair.

Wrapped in a warm spiritous dream deepened by several brandies it was merely natural that she should presently begin to make such remarks as 'heavenly, all this. Absolutely heavenly. I wouldn't have believed an evening could be so nice in this house. And all because of you.'

It was equally natural that she should presently turn to him, like a fire-drowsy cat, and rest her head against his knee, a gesture he accepted with a nervous tautness, not saying a word. The long silence that followed was merely blissful as far as she was concerned, but highly and tensely self-conscious on his part.

Suddenly he seized one of her hands, gripping and then caressing it with trembling eagerness. She treated all this with tolerant amusement. Even when he suddenly pressed his face against her hand and gave it a series of quick, broken kisses it never occurred to her that it might be the beginning of an exchange of affection.

Instead, in a spiritous haze that was still some way removed from actual drunkenness, she found herself feeling slightly sorry for him. Then, inconsequentially, she started teasing him in a light ardent sort of way.

'You're a very nice boy. I'll bet you have a thousand girls running after you.'

'No, no.'

'Oh! darling, of course you do.'

'One or two, sometimes, perhaps, but —'

'Don't tell fibs. I'll bet they all love you.'

'They're daft, most of them. Only half grown up.'

'I suppose you're going to tell me you really like older women? Do you? Naughty.'

He said nothing in answer to this and there followed another protracted, painful silence which she finally broke by saying:

'Pour me another brandy, darling. A nice big one. I like to feel it going round and round in me.'

Some time after this she began to lose control of her lips. She started slightly to slobber her words. Breaks of unsteady laughter punctuated her sentences and once as the spiritous hazy glow in her brain enlarged and deepened she remembered saying, playfully, with a bright giggle:

'All right, you can kiss me if you like. Just for this once I'll let you.'

There followed a moment or two of passionate ardour abruptly cut off, on his part, by a great convulsive sigh. She remembered feeling his hands at her breasts and then the entire heated trembling episode started to fade, leaving her body willingly exposed, her mind drowned in an enormously pleasurable half-consciousness.

Some hours later she woke, alone, cold, half-stripped, the fire completely out. Shivering, she felt fuddled and stricken with a dry shaking loneliness that lasted long after she had dragged herself to bed.

'Did you try to seduce me last night?'

They had been working for an hour or more on the kitchen the following morning when, cigarette in her nervous lips, she suddenly flung this question at him.

'Are you mad with me?'

'Oh! God, no. But a girl likes to be asked if she minds about these things.'

'You asked me.'

'Did I, by God? I can't remember.'

Half a minute later she suddenly did remember. A key abruptly clicked in her mind and she said:

'Oh! yes, I do now. It seems to me it wasn't very successful.'

He had nothing to say to this bruising remark, nor did it occur to her that it was something near to being a brutal one.

'If you're going to do these things, darling, you must learn to do them properly. It's an art, dear.'

He stood there unable to frame a single word. And then as if she suddenly realized that she had said something extraordinarily, impossibly insensitive she was again abruptly sorry for him and said:

'No, no, I didn't mean it quite like that. You were very sweet. But there's a way. Was I drunk?'

'I think you'd had –'

'I always think I'm a far nicer women when I'm drunk.'

'I think you're nice all the time.'

'Sweet boy, but a girl likes to be conscious when these things are going on.'

It never once occurred to her that such remarks could be construed as both affectionate and torturing. Completely changing the subject she suddenly said:

'I'll make some coffee. Oh! by the way I suppose you didn't get the lobster?'

No, he hadn't got the lobster. It had been too late for that. Tomorrow perhaps, he thought.

Painfully he stood staring at her with too-clear, too-brilliant eyes so that once again she was sorry for him and said:

'All right, you can kiss me if you like. That's what you want, isn't it?'

'That's how it began last night.'

'Yes, but this is morning. This is just friendly.'

He attempted to kiss her. She was amused, half-averted her face and suddenly turned away to make coffee.

'The snow's melting quite fast,' she said, 'I wonder if your skylark is singing again?'

He said he thought so; he'd heard it as early as nine o'clock as he came to the cottage.

'I don't think I'll have coffee after all,' she suddenly said. 'I'll have a drink instead. Just a sustainer.'

From that time until one o'clock she had several more sustainers. Gin after gin gave her a rosy, shallow, prattling air of affection. She became more and more warm and talkative, all trace of her normally querulous brittle manner gone.

'Are you coming in to see me every day? I wish you would, darling. I'll go crazy with one damn thing or another if I don't have you to talk to. What about the lobster? You promised the lobster. Would you cook it for me?'

Yes, he would cook the lobster for her, he said. But first, to get it, he'd have to run down on his mo-ped to the coast early in the afternoon. It would be too late when it got dark. He'd be gone an hour or two.

'Deserting me, are you? Leaving a girl in the lurch. Here am I all warm and cosy and you go off lobster hunting.'

'The man I get them from picks his pots up about half past two or three. If I don't get there –'

'I know, darling, I know. Choose two nice smallish ones, won't you? I think they're so much sweeter than the big fat ones.'

'Yes, Mrs Bartholomew.'

'And not Mrs Bartholomew, dear. My name's Stella.'

The very mention of her Christian name fired him into another attempt to kiss her. Again she half-averted her face.

'You must learn not to be so eager, darling. There's a time and place for everything. You hardly get the right atmosphere with a distemper brush in your hand.'

'I'm sorry, Mrs – I'm sorry.'

'Oh! don't be sorry. It's just that – like I say – there's a time and place for everything. Will it be dark by the time you get back?'

'I expect so.'

'I'll have a bath and put my house-coat on and make a nice big fire up. That's what I meant by time and place.'

His bewildered reception of all this was like that of a dog tormented by a bone cunningly flaunted just beyond his reach. The blue taunted eyes quivered with a degree of devotion that she found half-amusing, half-flattering.

'If I give you the money,' she said, 'will you bring some wine?'

'Oh! anything you like, Mrs – anything –'

'You're the sweetest lamb. You can kiss me now if you like. Just a little, little one.'

Spring came slowly and reluctantly to the marsh. By the very end of April certain stretches of the long grey dykes were at last gold with kingcups, with light feathery sweeps of lady-smock mauve between. An impassioned ceaseless song of skylarks filled the air. There came a day when she saw, for the first time, the blue and copper arrow of a kingfisher.

If her pleasure in seeing this transformation in a landscape she had once hated was great, that of Bartholomew was even greater. Every week-end he came down from town filled with fresh appetite for the pure marshland air, delighted at her conversion, at last, to the pleasure of the simple life. Her praises of Roger, the gem of a boy who could cook, wait at table, clip hedges, train roses, clean drains and generally impose transformations on the cottage she had once hated too, were doubly reflected in his own. It never occurred to him that he might be something more than a super manservant, youthfully eager to do nothing but serve.

'Oh! but so painfully shy,' she would say. 'Sometimes I hardly dare look at him it's so embarrassing. You know what he did one day? He picked up a thrush's egg that had fallen in the garden and brought it in to show me. You might have thought it was a jewel, a sapphire or something. It positively trembled in his hand.'

'He's done a great job on the garden,' Bartholomew said. 'I

could hardly believe he'd mown the lawn. And I tell you what –
I had an idea we'd paint the cottage walls white, you know
with that cement-cum-paint stuff. You think he could do that
too?'

'Oh! anything. You only have to ask him. He worships you.'

'Me?' This, Bartholomew thought, was engagingly funny. 'I
thought it was *you* he worshipped.'

'Oh! not me. Or if he does it's from far, far off.'

'Well, worship or not, the great thing is that you've really
started to like the place. Every week I expect to hear you're
bored with it all and every week you seem to like it more.'

'I must confess I was a bit hard on the marsh. In fact I loathed
it. But now that summer's practically here – Oh! there's a
funny, mysterious thing about the marsh. You don't get it for
a long time.'

A big old rose, long-neglected and suffocated by grass and
nettles, had by now been trained against the white west wall
of the house and by late June was covered with many flowers of
a rich, mellow creamy-rose.

On fine warm days she lay under this tree, on a foam mat-
tress, in a bikini, sheltered from the almost unused track beyond
the garden by a privet hedge neatly clipped to a height of five or
six feet. By this time sun and sea-air had begun to work a certain transformation in her too. Her skin had started to soften, to
lose at least some part of its uneasy, alcoholic snake-like tex-
ture. She was not only drinking less but had also grown out of
the habit of re-dyeing her hair every week or so in shades of
anything from yellow to a kind of brandy-rose. Its return to
natural colour also brought with it a comparable softness, so that
she looked much younger, very like a soft, furry, amber cat.

By this time the pleasure of teasing the boy, shallow though
it was, had slightly worn off. Not wholly bored, she nevertheless
started to find his presence about the place mildly irritating.
And one very hot July afternoon, in a deliberate attempt to re-
stimulate the amused pleasantries of the early acquaintance-
ship, she slipped off even the bikini and lay quite naked in the
sun.

She lay there for a good hour or more before gradually becoming aware that she was mildly irritated herself. For some reason the boy, she started to tell herself, wasn't coming back that afternoon. In growing irritation she realized that the surprise she had planned for him, the surprise of discovering her there in full nakedness under the rose tree, was a sort of poor joke that had failed. From across the marsh she heard one of its many church clocks strike three and then, some moments later, as if in echo, the slow funereal boom of a fog-horn.

The sound, mournful at any time, seemed even more like the moan of a dying animal in the hot July air. It mystified her that fog could possibly lie out at sea while she herself basked naked in the pure blissful heat of afternoon. Still further irritated, she found herself longing for the boy to be there, to touch her, caress her breasts, soothe her growing vexation and finally share her pleasure.

She heard four o'clock strike. A few minutes later the sun abruptly disappeared. A grey curtain of sea-fog drifted in and the air was suddenly damp and cold. She suddenly felt cold too and ran into the house to dress herself.

Dressed and imprisoned by fog, she mixed herself a stiff pink gin and gulped the greater part of it quickly. The lazy pleasure of the early afternoon had gone the way of the sun. She was again not merely irritated but querulous, cross, on the verge of being truculent. Every minute, after another gin or two, she became more and more loose-lipped, smoking in unsteady gasps, uneasily pacing about the rooms.

It was past five o'clock when she heard the stutter of the boy's small mo-ped coming up the track. That too merely served to irritate her and her voice was strident, even vicious, as she answered his call of 'May I come in?'

'Well, you bloody well know the way in, don't you? You should do by now.'

Coming into the sitting-room, he paused only a foot or two over the threshold, clearly nervous, as if about to apologize about something.

'I thought you were coming to trim the lawn? I had a surprise for you, a nice big juicy surprise. But forget it now. Where the hell did you get to?'

He started to explain that his mo-ped had gone wrong. He'd had to walk a couple of miles to a garage to get the necessary spare part and then back again and by the time –

'And then the bloody fog came in.' She suddenly laughed, partly against herself, softening. 'And me without a stitch on. You silly darling, why couldn't you have come? I was there waiting for you –' her voice was already dragging its words, slightly out of control – 'I wanted you to cook me – turn me over – get me brown all over –'

She sidled voluptuously against him, put both arms completely round him and in a voice growing more and more loosely lugubrious said she was sorry she'd spoken so sharply. But there were times when a girl wanted things, even wanted them badly, terribly badly. And one thing she'd always wanted was to get her breasts sun-tanned too, brown as the rest of her.

Just as men in moods of cold sobriety look on drunks with dispassionate embarrassment, seeing only objects of pathetic ridicule, he stood there statuesque, unmoved, not part of her mood and not knowing what to do.

'Have a drink,' she suddenly said. 'Warm you up after the fog. It's bloody cold, that fog. Warm you up. No use making love when you're cold – have to be warm – have a drink, darling. Let me –'

No, he said, he wouldn't have a drink. In fact it wasn't his intention to stay more than a few minutes anyway.

'Undress me. Here if you like. We'll use the settee – undress me, darling, here –'

Nervously he bit and licked his lips, clearly unable to find or frame the words he intended to say.

'What was that you said, darling? Not staying? Oh! but you are – now that I've got you here.' With groping fingers she started to unzip her dress, revealing smooth brown shoulders. 'See how marvellously brown I'm getting – want to get like that all over, every inch –'

The next thing she heard, and then at first not very clearly, was:

'I really came to tell you I wasn't coming any more. I got a job down at the power station. It's big money.'

With gin-soaked eyes she stared at him for fully half a minute, during which she tried several times to light a cigarette and each time failed hopelessly to bring lighter and cigarette together. Then she started laughing, nervously.

'Blast. You're going to *what*? Don't bloody well make me laugh. Of course you're coming again.'

She suddenly let her dress slip completely off and down to her ankles. Her exposed breasts, two paler cups in the almost acorn-brown of the rest of her body, stood out in invitation.

Stonily he resisted the invitation and then stuttered out a statement that first shattered and then infuriated her:

'I don't think it's fair to Mr Bartholomew.'

The sublime innocence of this sentence left her for a few moments impotent, utterly at a loss for any word, angry or otherwise. Then he opened his mouth to say something and she flew at him, bitterly:

'Who's talking about being fair? Oh! grow up. Be adult, for God's sake. We don't talk like that nowadays – it's fifty-fifty, isn't it? We're in it together. Who's talking about –'

'I still don't think it's fair to Mr Bartholomew. He's been very good to me.'

'Amazing conclusion to come to. Bloody amazing conclusion.'

'We ran down to the coast last Saturday afternoon while you were resting. He wants to buy a boat.'

'Oh! don't talk rubbish. Who the hell cares about boats?'

Suddenly she softened again. Laughing loosely, she lifted his hands to her breasts, guiding them into movements slow and caressive. His response to this was as cold as the sea-fog outside and her next words had a bitter whip in them:

'What in hell's the matter with you? It's like trying to rouse the dead.' The bitterness rose to a fearful stridency. 'But then you couldn't anyway, could you? You never even had one good short innings, let alone a long one, did you? Bowled first bloody

ball, every time. You never even once even remotely bloody well
made it –'

He stood shattered too, white-faced, unable to say a word.
The effect was to goad her into one final intolerable screech of
strident bitterness, half hysterical. Savagely covering her breasts
she whipped at him shrilly:

'Drop me a post-card one day. I'll pack them up and send
them to you. Registered. Cash on delivery, darling, cash on
delivery.'

The following week-end Bartholomew found her deep in a
mood of grey gloom and petulance, drinking as early as nine
o'clock in the morning, brain wandering, eyes as filmed as those
of a dying fish. Her talk was again inexplicably bitter and of
how she hated the bloody marsh, the bloody sea-fog, the fog-
horns, the herons, the grey dykes and above all the cottage and
being there alone.

'But where's Roger? Where's the boy?'

'Mr High-and-Mighty got too big for himself. Said I'd
offended him or some damn thing. Withdrawn his labour, as
they say. It's always the way with these people. You treat them
as equals and they spit on you.'

'I think that's a bit strong. He didn't by any chance make a
pass at you?'

'He couldn't make a pass at pussy.'

'Oh! we can't have this. This is ridiculous. The boy's always
been so friendly. There must be some explanation.'

'You go and seek it.'

'I think I must. We need him. He's made such an awful difference to the place. Besides, I hate bad feeling. And I must say
I've got awfully fond of the boy, in a way.'

'Congratulations.' Bitterness flowed again, unrestrained, shot
with the thinnest laughter. 'Tell him from me I'll write him a
reference. Strong, willing lad, paints, cooks, gardens, waits at
table, spits in your eye. And oh! by the way, what was all this
about buying a boat?'

Yes, Bartholomew said, he thought of buying a boat. He'd

always wanted to. Now that the cottage was all spick and span he rather wanted a new interest. And after all it seemed silly to be so near to the sea and not have a boat. It also seemed that the boy knew of one, fair-sized and pretty serviceable and not all that expensive.

'*Went to sea in a pea-green boat,*' she said. 'You'll go alone if you do. Boats are not for me. Boat me no boats.'

Once alone again, bitterness stifled, she nursed the absence of the boy with something very near to grief. With remorse she regretted everything she had said to him. Affection for him expressed itself in long cold spells of remorseless self-chastisement. A need for love found its answer in equally long gin-blind moods, grey and near to despair.

Bartholomew was late coming home that evening and she went to bed, securely drunk, without him, so that it was almost midday on Sunday morning before she was sober enough to ask:

'Well, did you see our late and unlamented Jack-of-all-trades?'

Yes, Bartholomew said, he'd seen him.

'And what about the boat? Did you buy the pea-green boat?'

They were, Bartholomew said, going to try it out that afternoon.

'And does it sail or has it got an engine? Or do you have to row, jolly old row?'

It had sails and an auxiliary.

'Needless to say the Jolly Roger will do all the work.'

Bartholomew now said that he wished she wouldn't talk like that. It wasn't fair on the boy. He'd talked to him yesterday for a long, long time and he'd got the impression that there was something big on his mind that he couldn't talk about. You might even say he was tortured about something in an odd sort of way.

'Calf-love, I expect. They get it at that age.'

Something more than that, Bartholomew thought. He divined somehow that it had something to do with her. He got an increasing impression that the boy thought he'd offended her and not the other way round.

'Like I told you,' she said, 'he couldn't offend pussy. I expect it's some tart goading him, some bird –'

He really thought he looked quite ill, Bartholomew said.

These last words affected her so much that she lay on her bed all afternoon, in a stupor of self-chastisement that brought her, at last, to tears. She ached to talk to the boy, to explain, to apologize, to redeem herself, to make for some better understanding. She was gripped, instead, by a dark self-pity and in the end, by evening, went back to drinking.

Bartholomew, returning home about eight o'clock, was a man as pleased with himself as a child with a brand new toy. He could speak of nothing but the boat, how she handled, the dream she was and the bargain, of how the boy would crew for him and how mightily competent, that afternoon, he had proved to be. Among all his other accomplishments he was now revealed as a damn good sailor.

'Learnt it all from one of the local fishermen. Old life-boat johnny. Taught him all the wrinkles. It's pretty tricky, this piece of coast. Hellish currents all over the show.'

Uninterested, she listened through a haze of alcohol.

'I'm so damned pleased with the thing,' Bartholomew said, 'that I've decided to take three weeks or a month off and really give her a thorough go. She's sea-going all right. Thought I'd call her *Sea Queen*.'

And what, she asked, did he call a thorough go? Where would he go?

'Roger says he's perfectly capable of taking her across the Channel and down the French coast. I thought we might even taken her up the Seine, say as far as Rouen.'

Well, he could count her out on that, she said. The simple life on shore was bad enough. But she wanted still less part of it at sea.

'The boy's never been abroad before. I thought it would be a great experience for him.'

Really? Hadn't there been, she said, some talk of his working at the power station? How was he arranging that?

'Oh! I talked him out of that. It isn't the job for him. He's an outdoor man. The sea and the marsh and all that – that's him.'

Oh! indeed? she said. He seemed all of a sudden, she thought, to have started to take an almighty strong interest in the boy.

'Well, frankly I have. I've got sort of attached to him.'

Attached? She seized on the word like an alcoholic tigress. And what the freezing hell did he mean by attached?

'He's very sensitive –'

Oh! indeed? How charming. And had the boy by any chance become attached too?

'I don't think it's a thing to be sarcastic about. He's going through a trying period – I feel tremendously in sympathy with him. He's awfully sensitive. He's all tangled up about something. I'd like to give him some understanding –'

Oh! let's all shed salt tears for the cabin boy, she said. Poor little cabin boy –

'That's pretty cheap,' he said, 'pretty low –'

And so he, she supposed, was the pretty boy? Was that it? It was all very touching. She could only hope they both enjoyed their long French honeymoon.

'I ought to belt you for that. But God help me, I doubt if you're even worth belting.'

No? she said. Then he could pour her a drink instead. A good long big whisky. Then she could wish him luck, good health, *bon voyage*, bless the bride and happy nights on honeymoon. God bless the *Sea Queen* and all who sail in her, while she stayed at home and burnt her bloody heart out.

Alone, on a day in August, she walked across the marsh, along the dykes. A keen wind, quite cold, was blowing in from the sea, ruffling and bending brown feathered reeds, pale lilac heads of marsh-mallow, purple torches of loose-strife. The many grazing sheep on the pastures were accompanied by white-grey flocks of gulls, feeding and spasmodically flying from one field to another. The towers of the power station, some distance down the coast, had the appearance of some curious castle, ancient but new, the colour of grey sand.

It was her intention to walk the four miles or so to the sea. She would, she felt, feel freer by the sea. A solitary imprisonment on the marsh, alone in the cottage, an entire month of the simple life, had become tolerable no longer. She had to walk, see the sea, acquaint herself with a new horizon.

Winter, as she had always felt it did, had once again begun in August. The voices of sea-gulls were harsh on the wind. There was a cold, clenching touch of salt in the air and ahead of her a heron rose from the dykes in slow flight, a grey ghost watching for prey.

The Four Beauties

I FIRST met the Davenports when they kept a little café behind the market square where, in a brief, highly unsuccessful and very painful spell of purgatory, I worked, or pretended to work, as a press reporter.

The little shop, not much more than fifteen feet square, was wedged behind a churchyard, between a row of solicitors' offices, a doctor's surgery and a religious bookshop, very much like a shabby orphan long since abandoned by the wayside and left there, unwanted and for ever unretrieved. Round the corner was the coroner's office and to this I dutifully went every morning to inquire if, by any chance, some unfortunate had been murdered, had committed suicide or come to some other untimely and perhaps violent end in the night. After this I called in on Mrs Davenport for a cup of tea, a poached egg on toast and sometimes an unusual sort of saffron cake, looking very much like a bright yellow toadstool.

Like her shop, Mrs Davenport, who was probably about thirty-nine, was slightly shabby. This is not to say that she was unwashed or in any way a slattern. She seemed merely to lack any kind of inspiration. The pinafore-smock she generally wore was clean enough but it always looked rather as if a restless and hairy horse had rolled on it for some considerable time. In the same way her dark hair was never quite in and never quite out of curlers. Somewhere she had simply lost heart about the business of either putting them in or taking them out again.

A little inspiration, or even a little lipstick, I always felt, would have worked miracles with Mrs Davenport, who was not only quite young and well-shaped but attractive in a doll-like way, but certainly none ever came from Mr Davenport. You never saw Mr Davenport in attendance at the steaming tea-geyser behind the counter; it was never he who came in from the back of the shop with the toast, the saffron cakes, the poached eggs or the plaice and chips. But sometimes a collarless, slightly balding, unshaven, jockey-like figure in shirt-sleeves skived sharply through the café like some swift and haunted malefactor on the run and slipped back again a few minutes later carrying a couple of bottles of stout and one of our racing extras.

But if Mrs Davenport had neither help nor inspiration from Mr Davenport she got a good deal from her three daughters, Tina, Sophie and Christabel. The most striking thing about the three girls was that they were not only beautiful, but beautiful in an utterly different way. Tina, the youngest, was fourteen and there were frequent moments when I, at twenty-two, felt quite elderly in her dark, delicate, impish presence. She had the eyes of a teasing, mischievous cat.

Sophie, at seventeen, was much more like a flower. Her blazing red hair always caused me to think of her as a tiger-lily. Perhaps it was also because she always wore it brushed into Turk's-cap curls, rather low in her long, honey-coloured neck. Her greenish sepia eyes were, strangely enough, not at all like those of a cat, when they clearly should have been. They had a deceptive limpidity that, until you knew her better, concealed a disarming – almost outrageous – way of changing expression, tone and colour, so that you never knew from one moment to another what mood lay behind them. You would see in them sometimes all the ardent, dreamy moodiness of someone deeply, even passionately, in love with you, only to have your hair madly ruffled a second later by the innocent fingers of a tomboy who not only hadn't the vaguest idea of what love was about but who hadn't an atom of femininity in her at all. She was, in fact, perhaps the most feminine of the three: elusive, intangible, infuriating and constantly giving the impression, in some odd way, of uneasy impermanence: as if, like a flower, her time of blossoming was not long.

When you came to Christabel, who was eighteen, you instantly felt you were in the presence of a character flamboyant but never in the least vulgar, a healthy lioness with golden eyes, hair the colour of oat straw and breasts of sensational splendour. Every strand of her hair and every pore of her smooth blonde skin radiated the feeling that she couldn't exist for a day without the food of love and that the richer and more bountiful the food the better. She was in fact the quietest of the three; the veins that seemed to diffuse that immoderate need for passion were often, in fact, tenderly, enchantingly sleepy.

These astonishing and disarming differences in the three sisters – it was almost as if Mrs Davenport, in various moments of desperate abandon, had gone off to seek solace in the arms of an Italian waiter, a red-headed Irishman and some giant athletic devotee of health-and-strength – were not only remarkable enough in themselves. They constantly made it impossible to believe that the girls had sprung from the shabby cradle of the little café, the slightly shabby Mrs Davenport and the even shabbier stout-addict whose sole interest in life seemed to be the racing results.

But the girls had still another characteristic, this time a similarity, which was also remarkable. All three were irrepressibly, almost unreasonably gay, with Christabel as the only one who sometimes slipped briefly into a drowsy minor key. Always as they came into the little café, giving Mrs Davenport a hand with the customers, there seemed to be in every poached egg a hidden secret joke; every saffron cake seemed to be leavened with laughter; not a single chip or pot of tea came in from the kitchen without the accompaniment of a sonata of giggles: so much so that I constantly felt that the little café would one day explode, evaporate into thin celestial air and, with its three beauties and their mother, vanish for ever.

And as it turned out I was, in a strange way, almost right about this.

One rainy evening in May, when the lilacs in the churchyard drooped flowers like wet pink sponges, I called in at the café about seven o'clock. Mrs Davenport never had any sort of regular closing time – sometimes she was open until eleven o'clock at night – but that evening she was already standing over the till, totting up the day's takings. There were no customers in the café and no sign at all of the girls.

'Oh! I'm sorry, Mrs Davenport. I didn't realize you were closing up.'

'Oh! that's all right. Sit yourself down. What can I get you?'

I really hadn't come with the intention of having anything, I said. I really wanted to speak to Christabel.

'They've all three gone to a film. It looked like being a long miserable wet evening and I packed them off. You know how they are. They like a little gaiety. I couldn't bear to have them moping. You say you wanted to speak to Christie?'

It was about a dance, I explained. I sometimes got free tickets for various occasions from the office. I now had two for the Golf Club dance the following Saturday and I wondered if Christie might come? That was if Mrs Davenport didn't mind and had no objection?

'Oh! she'd adore it. Mind? Of course I don't mind. My girls are free to enjoy themselves. They're not tied to the counter here.'

There was sometimes a certain reflective sadness in Mrs Davenport's voice and whenever it was there she drooped the lids of her eyes. I detected it now and I noticed too that she didn't look at me as she said:

'Do sit down, won't you? And can't I get you something? Some tea? I've got coffee already made.'

I thanked her and said I would like a cup of coffee. Rain beat in a sudden dark squall at the café window and she said, again in that sad voice, that she'd better put on the light. As she switched it on the naked brilliance of the bulb above the counter gave her something more than an air of sadness. She looked, I thought, in some way inexpressibly lonely, even troubled.

'Something to eat with it? Toast? or would you like a saffron cake? I baked them fresh this afternoon.'

I said I would have a saffron cake. She poured out a cup of coffee and put a saffron cake on a plate beside it. I spooned sugar into the coffee and as I did so she begged me once again to sit down.

'No,' I said, 'I'll stand and talk to you.'

Once again that reflective sadness spread across her face, giving it a distant air. Another squall of rain slashed at the window and then suddenly she said:

'Would you mind very much if I asked you something?'

'Of course not.'

It struck me suddenly that she was about to issue some sort of instruction as to my behaviour with Christie but instead she said:

'Do you like my saffron cakes? Honestly what do you think of them?'

'Oh! I like them. I always have.'

'I mean would you say they were something rather special? Very special?'

'I've certainly never come across them anywhere before. Why?'

She didn't answer my question. Instead she started to say that she made them from a very old recipe, from Norfolk, given to her by their old family cook.

'I was really rather like the girls in those days. Always teasing. I used to tease the coachman and the groom and the gardeners, everybody. Especially Cook. But she always let me copy out her recipes.'

The distant air on her face grew stronger. The veil of sadness showed no signs of lifting. Instead it was as if she had slightly opened a door, giving me a glance into another room in her mind.

'Why did you ask me about the cakes?'

Oh! yes, they were very well off in those days, she suddenly went on to say. Then her father got killed when a carriage and pair bolted. Not long afterwards her mother got tied up with a waster and suddenly everything started to go to pot. At eighteen, in desperation to get away from it all, she married Davenport, one of the grooms.

Once again I asked her about the cakes but again she didn't bother to answer.

'I expect I'm boring you to death, but tell me something. Supposing you were sort of trapped and you suddenly had the chance to get away. Say in your job. Do you like your job or not?'

'I loathe it.'

'Why don't you leave?'

'I'm going to. It's mad, I suppose. I've got nothing else –'

'Of course it's mad. But you won't be in the trap, will you?'

Slowly she folded her arms on the counter and for the first time looked clearly and directly at me. Her eyes, like Tina's, were a dark clear brown. The air of sadness had considerably lifted now but it was still hard to believe that somewhere far behind the clear brown pupils another Tina had once existed, teasing, impudent and gay.

'Well, it's like this. Or am I boring you?'

'Far from it.'

A couple of weeks before, she said, a traveller from one of the big biscuit firms had dropped in at the café. He ordered a pot of tea and then proceeded to go quietly mad about the saffron cakes. They were so good he was convinced she ought to market them: advertise them, set up a mail order business or something, get a traveller to push them around the shops. That was the way big things began. A little old lady started to make old-fashioned mint humbugs in a back kitchen, or marmalade, or almond rock, or gingerbread, and suddenly somebody took it up and in ten years it was a household word and they were quoting shares.

'Sounds fine. But you'd need capital.'

'Exactly. I told him that. And there isn't any capital. Or wasn't. Until today.'

Yes, he'd been in again that very afternoon, so convinced he was right that he'd got the capital all arranged. He was sure she couldn't go wrong. She could pay it all back with interest over three or four years.

To my infinite astonishment I saw her smile. This sudden turn of brightness, almost a blossoming, made me realize for the first time how young after all she was. With that sudden smile some of her shabbiness dropped away. I even told myself that I half-detected, in the bright brown pupils, the remotest reflection if not of Tina's impish impudence, at least a slight awakening.

'Have you made up your mind?'

'Not quite. I'm going to sleep on it. He'll be in again on Saturday.'

It was now almost dark outside. The sky was a strange brilliant electric blue and I thought the rain had stopped.

'I ought to get back to the office,' I said. 'Will you ask Christie about the dance? You think she'd like to come?'

'Of course. She'll adore it.'

'The dance starts at eight. I'll call for her just before.'

She actually smiled again, not briefly this time but broadly, so that I suddenly realized how pretty, underneath that veil of shabby sadness, she really was.

'I warn you, though. The other two will be raving jealous mad.'

A minute later I said good night to her and walked across the churchyard. The rain had stopped. In the deepening twilight big fat drops of it were falling from heavy sprays of lilac, splashing on the tombstones below.

One of the more curious things about the Davenports was the way, in the presence of one, I would be haunted by the absence of another. For some days I was haunted by Mrs Davenport; there was something strangely discomforting about that talk of ours in the café. But it was nothing to the way, shortly afterwards, I was to be haunted by Tina.

When I called for Christabel on Saturday evening Mrs Davenport was busy serving half a dozen customers in the café and there was a sound of music from the room in the back.

'I don't think Christie's quite ready yet,' she said. 'She always takes an age. Anyway go through to the living-room and sit yourself down in comfort. Tina's there.'

When I went through to the back room Tina was dancing round the table to the tune of a fox-trot being played on a portable gramophone. Her arms were holding an imaginary partner and her dark head was thrown well back, so that her bare neck looked sleek and long. For some reason I also thought she looked older than usual and it was some time before I discovered why.

'I'm having my own private dance,' she said. Impetuously she stretched out her arms and held me by the shoulders, the very dark bright eyes fixed on me in an impish open stare. 'Will you have the pleasure?'

I held her by the waist and she responded by putting a bare arm lightly but caressingly across my shoulders. This deliberate gesture of intimacy had the immediate effect of sending a series of brittle electric waves through my spine. But it also had another odd and unexpected effect. I suddenly found myself uneasy, almost half-frightened: not merely because she was so young but because, in spite of it, she was also so disturbingly, even alarmingly, mature.

'Come on, dance,' she said. 'You're like a wooden horse.'

Then, as we danced, I suddenly discovered the reason for my thinking that she looked so much older than she really was. She was wearing a dress at least a couple of sizes too tight for her and it struck me all at once that this too was a deliberate gesture. The dress, cut rather low at the neck, was of emerald green chiffon – she might well have worn it for her birthday party a year before – and its tightness had the effect of throwing her bust into firm, tender and very startling prominence. It was almost as if her young breasts, though by no means as striking in form as Christie's, had miraculously matured in the day or two since I had seen her before. The effect of them was sensational.

In this bemused state of amazement and half-fear I hadn't the vaguest idea what to say to her. Then the side of the gramophone record came to an end and she released herself from me and went across the room to turn it over. The gramophone was standing on a low bamboo coffee table by the window and as she deliberately bent deeply over it I caught a glimpse of the shadowy hollow between her breasts. Almost at once, knowing perfectly well I was staring at her, she looked up, unabashed, and calmly said something about it being a waltz on the other side.

I said I was afraid I really didn't waltz all that well and she at once said:

'That won't suit Christie. She adores waltzing. It's her favourite dance. Anyway I think you're an awful old pig. You might have taken me.'

I murmured something about her being a little on the young side, perhaps, and she said: 'Oh! nonsense. Someone told me the other day I look at least seventeen.' She deliberately straightened herself up to her full height, arching her bust, once again holding me in that frank, dark gaze of hers. 'Do you think I do?'

In that moment I was bound to admit that she did. A little later the music started again and once more she came across and to my infinite embarrassment laid that bare, caressive arm on my shoulder.

'You only asked Christie just to make me jealous. Promise me you'll take me next time you get tickets.'

'I shan't get any more tickets. I'm leaving the paper next week.'

'If you're hard up I can pay for myself.'

'It isn't anything to do with being hard up. It's – well –'

'It's – well, what?'

'You may look seventeen but in fact you're only fourteen. You're still at school. It's a bit much.'

'Oh! it's a bit much, is it? Thank you.'

'I'm sorry, I didn't mean it like that.'

'Oh! you're sorry, are you? Well, I'll forgive you if you promise to take me next time.'

More out of renewed fear than anything else I hastily promised I would take her next time and as an immediate gesture of gratitude she kissed me full on the lips, and not with casual lightness either. If the sudden revelation of her maturing breasts had an air of the miraculous about it that first kiss of hers was even more sensationally so. It had in it all the rare ardour of a girl long practised in the pursuits of love.

'We must do that again some time,' she said. 'Christie's just coming down.'

In that moment I had never been quite so relieved to see any-one as I was to see Christie. She was wearing a pale primrose dance frock, with a lime green wrap and a double row of pearls. There was never a time when the Davenport girls looked any-thing but striking but that evening Christie looked so supremely lovely that I was filled with an entirely fresh rush of embarrass-ment, this time born of sheer wonder.

'Don't care much for the pearls. They don't go with that frock.'

'No? Well, nobody asked *you* to wear them.'

'Good thing, too. Jewellery doesn't suit me either.'

Christie didn't say a word in answer. Instead she simply turned to me and said:

'Shall we go? I'm sorry if I've been rather a long time but I had a bit of trouble with the zip of my dress. It really isn't quite right even now. Of course it would help if some people – do it up for me, will you?'

She turned her back towards me and I saw that the zip of her dress was still open a couple of inches from the top. As I moved to touch it a dark shadow marched across the room. It was Tina, in fiery departure.

'Don't let him ask you to waltz. He doesn't do it very well.'

'Thanks for telling me. But I think,' Christie said, 'we are old enough to please ourselves.'

All that sultry May evening I danced physically with Christie, but in spirit with Tina. That special quality of the Davenports, of being able to haunt in absence, was so manifestly strong that several times I only saved myself by the sheerest miracle from calling the girl in the pale primrose dress by the wrong name.

The evening had begun by her going to the ladies' room and coming back without her pearls. When I remarked on this she said:

'I really didn't think they suited me after all. She's nearly always right, Tina. She's got taste, that child.'

'I'm sorry you're not wearing them. I thought they looked marvellous. Won't you put them on again?'

'No, I don't think so.'

Then later, as we were having supper of ham sandwiches, coffee and, believe it or not, raspberry jelly and cream, she suddenly took off her bracelet – it was a simple gold affair with a single locket attached – and said:

'I don't think I'll wear my bracelet either. It keeps half-slipping off anyway. Put it in your pocket, will you?'

I duly put the bracelet into my pocket and promptly forgot it. Somehow she looked only half-dressed with neither pearls nor bracelet and again I said:

'I really do think the pearls suit you. Won't you wear them after supper?'

She clearly must have felt flattered by this, because just before we began dancing again she went away to the ladies' room and came back, some ten minutes later, wearing the necklace. I at once said how charming the pearls looked and again how much they suited her and in return she gave me the warmest of responses with those large golden eyes of hers.

For a girl with such a big and splendid body Christie danced with amazing lightness. She was as light as a fresh-made meringue and the feeling she gave with it was similarly cool and sweet. Mistakenly, as it turned out, I at first found her beauty that night to be neutral and unexciting. Perhaps it was the continually tumultuous recollection of that dark and precocious kiss of Tina's that was responsible for this but it became clearer and clearer, the more we danced, that my interpretation of her as an impassioned creature insatiably hungry for the food of love was a mistaken one. The lioness was gorgeous but tame.

'Don't you really waltz?' I had already excused myself from one waltz and was really half-dreading another. 'Or is it just that you don't like it?'

'I don't do it very well and I don't want to make an ass of myself. Or stamp on your toes.'

'That's all right. Then you won't mind if I dance the next one with George Parkinson, will you? He asked me at the interval.'

'Of course not.' I knew George as a gayish sort of man with strong hunting instincts where girls were concerned and I added: 'You'd just better buckle on your armour all the same.'

'Oh! George is as harmless as a worm. I've danced with him before.'

'Worm? I've always heard he was something of a scorpion.'

'Oh! not George. You're as safe as houses with George.'

I suppose I ought to have experienced some slight pang of jealousy as she went off to waltz with George but, again perhaps because of that urgent and recurrent recollection of Tina, I felt not the slightest twinge of one.

Instead I took the opportunity of going outside for a breath or two of night air. The dance was being held at one of those big old manor houses converted into a road-house and the gardens of it stretched away towards a river. I was afterwards to have more than ordinary cause to remember that river but that night I simply stood under a great chestnut tree – almost all its blossom had fallen and lay underneath it like scattered snow in the lights of the house – and breathed the warm early summer air. There was none of the malice of May in that evening and even the stars, everywhere visible in crowds beyond the tips of a big row of poplar spires, looked warm.

And again it was of Tina, not Christie, that I thought as I stood in solitary contemplation of the night sky. All men, I suppose, dream at some time or other of being kissed by a strange woman, only to wake up, empty-lipped, at the supreme climax of its excitement. And now it began to be like this with Tina. That impulsive kiss of hers began to assume far more than the mere pleasure of an exquisite surprise. It too became a dark dream from which I had been rudely snatched away, a haunting myth that gave as much pain as pleasure because it seemed, really, never to have happened.

But the night still had yet another surprise for me. When I got back to the dance floor and found Christie again I said:

'It's a simply marvellous warm night. Should we walk home across the meadows?'

'But it must be all of two miles.'

'There's a footpath. It comes out at that old stone bridge. I know the way. How did the waltz go?'

'Lovely. You weren't jealous, were you, because I danced with George?'

'Not a scrap.'

For fully a quarter of a minute those large golden eyes of hers held me in gentle and slightly mocking reproach.

'That, I think,' she said, 'was not very flattering.'

I apologized and said that, of course, it wasn't. Typically thoughtless of me.

'I wouldn't have said you were thoughtless.'

'Oh! well, it doesn't matter. Shall we walk back across the meadows?'

'If you think you know the way.'

'We'll navigate by the stars.'

As it turned out it wasn't necessary, as we started to walk home just after midnight, to navigate by the stars. The footpath was clear in the light of them. As we walked I put my arm round her waist, my hand under her right breast. We didn't talk very much but after about five minutes, half way across the first meadow, I stopped and kissed her.

In my mistaken belief that she was, after all, unimpassioned, a mere girlish meringue at once cool and sweet, I made the kiss of, as I thought, appropriate lightness. To my infinite surprise she responded with an amazing and mature tenacity, at the same time lifting one of my hands deliberately to her breast. An instant later I was suddenly aware that she was all vibration. I began trembling myself and all of a sudden, in a dynamically charged moment that even Tina couldn't have matched, we half-fell, half-stumbled to the ground.

How long we lay there I haven't the remotest idea; but some long time later she extracted herself from my embrace and then folded her body like a big warm quilt over mine, her bare breasts against my face.

'I have,' she said, 'something to tell you.'

'Oh! God, not now. Words, words – please – not words.'

'I've been wanting to tell you all evening but I didn't want to spoil it.'

'Spoil it! And you choose a moment like this. God, is it so important?'

'Of course it is. Otherwise I wouldn't tell you. Listen.'

'You expect a man to listen in an attitude like this?'

'Listen.'

It isn't all that easy to listen, rationally at any rate, when you are being held in a dark meadow, on a warm May night, by a lioness you hitherto thought was tame and is now disturbingly, passionately transfigured; but somehow, in that whirl of emotion, I listened and I heard her say:

'I'm going away.'

'What a moment to tell me!'

'Don't sound so tragic.'

'But where? When? You mean for good?'

She suddenly laughed gaily, in the true Davenport way, and said:

'Oh! good gracious, no. Just for a couple of weeks. On holiday. Liz Davidson has an aunt who keeps a boarding house down at Brighton. You know Liz – she works with me. We can stay for practically nothing – it's too good to miss –'

'Oh! Christie, don't go, don't go. For God's sake don't go. Not after this.'

'Of course I shall go.'

'God,' I said, 'I'll hate you if you go.'

An instant later she was on her feet, hands furiously struggling to straighten the front of her dress. It was the first and only time I ever saw her in a temper, almost a rage, and I was just preparing myself for a blast of words that would banish me for ever when suddenly her hand accidentally caught at her necklace. The string broke. There was a little explosive tinkle as the pearls scattered over her bare breasts and down the primrose dance frock, both inside and outside, to the grass below.

A moment later we were lying on the ground again, helpless with laughter.

Three evenings later I went round to the little café, having at last remembered Christie's bracelet. Again Mrs Davenport was alone behind the counter and again, I thought, she wore that slightly sad, slightly distant air.

'Oh! the bracelet – she hoped you'd bring it in before she went away.'

A pang of disappointment nipped sharply at my heart, so that for a moment I hadn't anything to say. Finally I apologized and then explained that I'd been to London for a couple of days, half in the hope of getting another job.

'And did you?'

I said I hadn't and that if the truth had to be told, I hadn't tried very hard.

'I think she was disappointed you didn't come in. I'm afraid Tina isn't here either and Sophie's upstairs, scribbling away at letters. She's great on sending for catalogues, our Sophie. They arrive by the cart-load. So I'm afraid there's only dull old me to talk to.'

She then asked me if I'd like a coffee and having said I would I leaned my elbows on the counter and said:

'I didn't think Christie was going for another week. As a matter of fact I half-thought that it was you who'd have gone away.'

'What on earth made you think that?'

'Your scheme. Have you done anything about it?'

She at once confessed she hadn't. She didn't really know why, except that she'd been rather extra busy for the last several days. Her voice was vague. A listlessness in her dark eyes accentuated, as it so often did, that lack of inspiration I so often found in her. Even when she poured out two cups of coffee it was with an air so absent and purposeless that finally she lost her grip on what she was doing and let the second cup brim completely over.

'Sorry. Clumsy of me.' She slowly poured the spilt coffee from the saucer into another cup, pushed the sugar-basin across the counter and wiped her hands across her apron. At no time had I seen her look less like the mother of those three so different, dazzling beauties. 'No, I've slept on it a good bit, but I can't somehow make up my mind.'

'What do the girls say?'

Oh! she hadn't told the girls. She hadn't said a word to them. In fact I was the only living soul she'd spoken to.

'And why did you tell me?'

It was somehow easier to tell a – she seemed, I thought, about to use the word stranger, but after a brief pause she went on and said simply a person outside the family. And a man too. It was altogether easier, somehow, to confide in a man.

'It sounds to me like a golden opportunity,' I said. 'What holds you back?'

'Oh! me. Just me. I simply need a thorough good push.'

'Just the inspiration.'

'Inspiration?' She gave a short, completely mirthless laugh and cast an equally sombre look round the café and said: 'Here? Inspiration? You can see it growing up the walls, can't you? Like thick red roses.'

Hitherto she had been merely lifeless, vague, distant, disenchanted or just shabbily sad, but never bitter. Now the sentence about thick red roses was bitter: so bitter that it prompted me to say:

'Remember the trap? Well, I've got out of it.'

'Oh! yes, I'm good at giving advice. To other people. I just lack the urge to give it to myself.'

'Oh! go!' I suddenly said. 'Stand not upon the order of your going but go at once! Before it's too late! –'

No doubt this sounded a little over-dramatic but I really meant it as the verbal equivalent of shaking her. For several moments she looked extraordinarily startled. There was actually a flash of light in her eyes and for a second or two I thought that, like Christie, she was about to turn on me in anger. Nothing of the kind happened and in a few moments she was her distant, disenchanted self again.

'Of course you're quite right,' she said. 'I know that. And I'll tell you this. If I ever do make the plunge it'll be because of what you've just said.'

I was just beginning to nurse an uneasy feeling of embarrassment about all this when suddenly Sophie came into the café, dressed in an emerald green woollen jumper and a darker skirt, carrying a handful of letters. There was already a touch of dusk in the air and that brilliant tiger-lily head of hers glowed in the shadowy recesses of the café like a torch. Against the huddled figure of her mother, bent over the coffee cup, she looked like a goddess, more outrageously beautiful than Christie, more alarming than Tina, so that my blood started bumping and dancing. I suppose I'd seen her standing there in the café fifty times or more but that dusky late May evening it was incredibly as if I were seeing her for the first time.

'Oh! it's you. I wondered who was talking. I thought you'd deserted us.'

'That,' I said, 'I shall never do.'

She laughed with the typical Davenport gaiety, slightly mockingly.

'Doesn't he know how to say the right things? It's a pity you didn't save that for Christie. It might have been a bit of comfort for her.'

'You'd better look out,' Mrs Davenport said, actually smiling at me. 'She's in one of those moods. She'll tease the life out of you.'

'In which case,' I said, 'I'd better go. May I post your letters?'

'No. Thanks all the same. If you're going I'll walk as far as the post with you. That is if the strain of a Davenport companion isn't too much for you.'

This, I realized, was a reference to Christie, whom it would appear I had deserted, and once again came the warning from Mrs Davenport to watch my step. Sophie was in one of those merciless moods.

After saying good night to Mrs Davenport, Sophie and I started walking through the churchyard. The lilacs were all over now but in the breathless dusk a huge late magnolia held a thousand ethereal candles against the funereal column of an Irish yew. We stopped for a moment or two to gaze at it,

Sophie's head like fire against the pure crowd of blossom, and then we walked on.

'I can't think why you always walk so fast,' she suddenly said. 'You stride out as if you haven't a minute to live. Now slow down.' She caught at my arm. 'There's no hurry, is there? We've got all the time in the world.'

She was quite right. There was no hurry; we had all the time in the world; and slowly we walked through the church-yard and out into the market square beyond. Behind us the church clock chimed four quarters and then struck nine and as Sophie dropped her letters into the pillar box on the corner of the square I said:

'Are you going straight back or –'

'It all depends if I hear of any fascinating alternatives.'

'And which form would you prefer them to take?'

If she could banter, so could I. It might well be difficult to keep up with the spirited flash and change of the mind that lay behind the restless sepia-green eyes but that too was a pursuit also fascinating.

'Walk as far as the river?'

'Ah! you've got the river on your mind again.'

'Again? I don't know what you mean.'

'You know what I mean.'

Abruptly, and I thought prudently, I changed the subject.

'Did Christie arrive safely?'

'If it isn't the river it's Christie. I suppose they go together.'

'Brighton's nice. I went there twice as a boy.'

'Christie says so too. We had a card. She says I should go down for the day.'

'And will you?'

'If I could get an escort.'

'I'll escort. Decently.'

'And I, I suppose,' she said, 'will play the dear, dear goose-berry.'

In this sharp, light-hearted fashion we bantered our way to-wards the river, Sophie sometimes innocently inconsequent, sometimes a creature of complex maturity, and I all the time not knowing, in my own peculiar innocence, that I was about to make a new discovery about her: namely that she was not only very beautiful but, in the nicest sort of way, the most tormenting and beautiful liar.

Just as in the physical presence of Christie I had found myself uneasily in spirit with Tina, so in the presence of Sophie I now found myself thrown back, as it were, into the arms of Christie. There was no accident in this. Sophie was determined that I should; it was her avowed intention to torment me.

We had reached the bridge over the river and were standing in one of its triangular stone recesses, gazing down at a strong current foaming through the arches, the dark water full of stars, when all at once she said, with the most casual innocence:

'I heard all about Saturday.'

For a moment I didn't know whether to be shocked, annoyed or merely dismayed, but one thing was quite certain: I was once again lying in the meadow with Christie, kissing her splendid breasts in the cool air of early morning, and the recollection of it was all highly disturbing.

'*All* about Saturday?'

'Well, all that really mattered. You know, all the best bits.'

'I'm very glad to hear it. I wouldn't want you to miss a thing.'

'It must have been pretty terrific. I mean the way Christie described it.'

'Good God, you don't mean – look, haven't you sisters any secrets from each other?'

'Oh! don't sound so innocent.'

'I am not,' I said, 'trying to be innocent. But after all there are certain things –'

Immediately she threw back her lovely tiger-lily head and laughed mockingly into my face, her white teeth glistening.

'Anyone might think,' she said, 'that you were the only person who'd ever made love.'

She had been leaning on the parapet by the bridge, elbows crooked, and now she suddenly turned and gave me a look of searching warmth that couldn't be construed as anything but the most ardent invitation to kiss her. I promptly moved forward to do so, only to find her two hands squarely pressed against my chest, keeping me away.

'Oh! no you don't.'

'Don't you want to be kissed?'

'I'm not sure. I'll think about it.'

'Kissing,' I said, 'is not something you think about. You do it. On impulse. And it's very nice. Sometimes.'

'And what was "sometimes" supposed to mean?'

'You can hardly judge the quality of a kiss if you're not even given the chance of testing it,' I said, 'can you?'

She could apparently think of nothing to say in answer to this remark and I got some momentary satisfaction out of feeling that the exchanges had, so far, been fairly even; but suddenly, in a flashing change of subject, she was again ahead of me.

'I suppose you know that she's really in love with a man named Bill Cartwright?'

'And who is she?'

'Christie.'

I must confess I felt rather sick. There was in fact not the slightest need to have done so, since the remark about Bill Cartwright was, as I later discovered from Christie, merely another charming, blatant lie. Nor was the implied suggestion that she was a frequent lover herself any nearer the truth; she had up to that time never made love in her life, except in the deep, dark recesses of her mind.

'You don't seem to be terribly jealous about it,' she suddenly said.

'Am I supposed to be jealous?'

'Well, I should have thought it was a perfectly natural thing for a man who's in love with her.'

'Who said I was in love with her?'

'Well, aren't you?'

'I'm not sure. Perhaps I prefer someone else.'

'And who, might one ask, would she be?'

'That,' I said, 'would be telling.'

She leaned back against the bridge, deliberately arching her body, so that the curves of it were thrown forward, tightened.

'Oh! you do fancy yourself, don't you? First you get Tina on the hop. Then it's Christie. Now it's some mystery woman you've found.'

Suddenly, in the middle of all this nonsense – I don't know why, perhaps it arose in some way from the deep suspense of the night air about the dark river, where a white patch or two of mist had started to gather – I was troubled by the strange thought I sometimes had about her: that that flower-like loveliness of hers was somehow uneasy, fragile, doomed to impermanence. It made me for a second or two rather sad and then she said:

'What is she like? Some raging beauty I expect? Do I know her?'

'Ravishing. Oh! yes, you do.'

'Describe.'

'Marvellous figure. In fact, has everything.'

'Don't tell me she has bow-legs, too.'

'About seventeen. Gorgeous red hair. Lovely green-brown eyes –'

A second later, on one of those infuriating impulses of hers, she was ruffling my hair with both hands. She even thumped a knee into my thigh.

'Beast. Wretch. Skunk –'

'You said describe –'

'I loathe you. I hate you.'

'In that case I'd better start walking home.'

'It would be much easier,' she said, 'to jump into the river.'

I said I was afraid I couldn't swim and suddenly, in the flash of a second, her mood had changed. She actually stood there and smoothed my hair back into place with her two hands and looked at me with eyes at once tender and amazed.

'You're having me on. *You can't swim?*'

'Never liked water. Do you swim?'

'I'm mad about it. Crazy. That's one reason why I want to

go down to Brighton. I've never swum in the sea. Would you come too? I could teach you. Promise you'll come. Next Saturday.'

She was so suddenly full of friendliness and warmth and sheer sweetness that I in turn was filled with a new affection for her, a quite serious wave of tenderness.

'I'll promise,' I said, 'if you'll let me kiss you.'

'Oh! no thank you. I'm not open to bribes.'

Abruptly the mood was changed and shattered again. My moment of tender affection snapped into sharp annoyance. I was suddenly irritated by dalliance, tired of being kept on a string.

'I think,' I said, 'I'd better go.'

'Alone? Or could you bear my company?'

'As long as it's silent. Yes.'

So we started to walk home in silence, I stubborn in frustration. I ought to have known that no mood of hers would last very long but I was determined, this time, that no word of mine should break it. And suddenly it was she who broke it, as I should have known she would, by stopping outside the iron gates of a largish stone house and saying with an air of casual innocence that concealed yet another charming lie:

'This is my uncle's house. It's nice, isn't it?'

'I didn't know you had an uncle.'

'Oh! yes. He lives here. What are those white flowers?'

Even in the summer darkness I could detect a line of short white flowers fringing a path on the other side of the gates and I said I thought they were white pinks. There were no lights to be seen in the house windows and suddenly she said:

'Go and pick me a bunch. Go on.'

'I am not,' I said, 'in the habit of stealing flowers from other people's gardens.'

'Don't be priggish. This is different.'

'I am not being priggish and how is it different?'

'It's my uncle's garden.'

'Then go and ask him for some.'

'He isn't there. He's away on holiday.'

'Then you pick some.'

'You're such a coward.' Again she laughed in my face, throwing back her thick curled tawny hair. 'Do I have to dare you to? Or bribe you? Or what?'

I said that, like her, I wasn't open to bribes and immediately she said:

'Do you still want to kiss me?'

'Oh! all right, damn you.'

It was characteristic of the Davenports that sooner or later they cajoled, tricked or mesmerized you into doing things you knew perfectly well were impossible, illogical or just plain mad. I believe if Sophie had suddenly asked me, on that warm June night, to catch the midnight train and run away with her I might well have done so without even considering the consequences of abduction. In the same way I suddenly pushed open the garden gate and stepped inside to pick the flowers.

Suddenly a dog began barking. I was half in hurried retreat when she sharply pushed me back. It was only a poodle, I heard her say, one of those toy things. To me it sounded infinitely more like the venomous growlings of some immense mastiff in the early stages of hostile rage and I instantly started to retreat again, saying:

'For God's sake let's get out of here. Quick.'

So I was afraid of a little dog, was I? What a man.

'I am not afraid of little dogs but I am not particularly keen on being torn limb from limb.'

'Scared of a little yapping.'

Instantaneously the dog opened its lungs full blast to the night air with a bark of such reverberating savagery that I hastily shut the gate. She promptly pushed it open again, at the same time pushing me.

'Just make a dash for it.' The dog was silent now and the silence was of a chill uncanniness more forbidding than any sound of rage. I began to feel, in fact, slightly unwell. I profoundly wished I was lying in some quiet meadow with only the passionate bosom of Christie to disturb me and then suddenly she pushed me once more and I was in the garden again. 'Go on. Just a small bunch. It won't take a second.'

All of a sudden it seemed like having a tooth out; I might just as well, I thought, get it over with; and still in that uncanny silence I started up the path. The pinks were thick and white in the beds on either side of the path and with a feeling of guilt that was also in a curious way uncommonly and painfully exciting I hastily bent down and started to pick among them.

Abruptly another monstrously reverberating roar hit the night air and I turned, with a mere half dozen pinks in my hand, to see a black shape of terrifying proportions, as big as a bear it seemed, bounding at me up the path.

Utterly convinced that I was about to be laid on the altar of some savage sacrifice, I ran, clashing the gate shut behind me. By this time Sophie was running too. A second later a man's voice started shouting 'Who's there? Who the devil's there?' but the only answer it got was a chain of irrepressible peals of Sophie's laughter as she tore up the road, her red hair flying out in a Bacchanalian skein behind her.

She was still being consumed by occasional fits of laughter when we got to the churchyard. I even laughed myself once or twice, out of sheer relief, as you so often do in the blessed aftermath of fright or danger. Nor is the word blessed an accidental one. In the quietness of the churchyard everything seemed exactly that: the summer grass between the white headstones, the clover scent of pinks, a street lamp shining at the far end of the church path and in turn the lamps of the big magnolia themselves shining, purest white, in the night air.

For some long time we sat on one of the stone seats inside the porch of the church. All excitement spent, she was calm and quiet now too, no longer tempestuous or tormenting. Affectionately I smoothed her thick hair and finally took her in my arms and kissed her. She was, surprisingly, less demanding than Christie and I was very glad of it. That night I needed kisses of a nature more soothing than sensuous and it was these she gave me, embracing me in a vacuum that might have been virginal, and indeed was. In return and in gratitude I told her I loved her, though I really didn't, and she in turn, with that obligingly sweet side of her nature that sometimes counteracted the infuriating and inconsequent in her, told me she loved me, though that too was merely another charming, beautiful, forgivable lie.

'What time do we go to Brighton on Saturday?'

'I looked up a train,' she said. 'There's one at five past ten. Would that suit you?'

I said it would and she said:

'Good. We'll have a lovely day. We'll have lots of fish and chips and I'll teach you to swim.'

'I'll probably sink like a stone,' I said and a second later wished, as I still wish now, that I'd never said it.

I should have known that we would never get to Brighton: that some inconsequential change of mood in Sophie would, like a hurricane, speedily gust so simple and straightforward a plan away. I should have known too, if I had thought about it at all, that she hadn't the remotest intention of sharing me with Christie.

When I went round to the little café about a quarter to ten on Saturday morning Mrs Davenport was alone there except for two bus drivers having tea and sausage rolls at a table by the window. I heard one of the busmen say he'd bet his best hat it was going to be the hottest day of the year, it was sweltering already, and then Mrs Davenport said:

'I'm afraid my girls are always keeping you waiting. Sophie isn't quite ready.'

'We mustn't miss the train.'

She didn't say anything to this. Then I noticed that she was packing a rather big rush basket with food: meat pies, bananas, cheese, a loaf, butter, hard-boiled eggs, watercress and so on. Finally she put a big bottle of lime juice into the basket and I said:

'It rather looks as if someone is going for a picnic.'

'You are.'

'Oh! this is for the beach at Brighton?'

'No, no, she doesn't want to go to Brighton after all.'

'Why ever not?'

'For one thing she thinks it's too hot. And for another it's too far. And I must say I'm inclined to agree with her.'

'Where does she want to go?'

'She'll tell you.'

While I was pondering on the possibility of Sophie being in a mood more than usually fickle and elusive, Tina came into the café from the back room. I immediately said 'Hullo' to her but she didn't say a word in answer. There was an extraordinarily strange look on her face: disturbing and hard to define. She looked partly as if she hadn't slept very well and partly as if she were the victim of some self-afflicted confusion. She had lost all trace of mischief and impishness. Her mouth was set. A dark and distant air not unlike that I sometimes detected in her mother gave her a touch of near-bitterness intolerable in someone so young. Defensively she glowered not at me, but through and past me.

'I think you might say good morning to people when they speak to you,' Mrs Davenport said.

Far from saying 'Good morning' or indeed anything else the youngest of the Davenports merely gave me another glower that I can only describe as old in female contempt, turned on her heel and disappeared into the back room.

'What on earth is the matter with Tina?'

'If you gave me all the tea in China I couldn't tell you.'

'She's usually so gay.'

'Not today she isn't. Not today.'

Five minutes later Sophie came into the café carrying a towel and a yellow swim-suit, which she put into the picnic basket. She had evidently washed her hair the previous night and now it shone more than ever brightly, with the tiger-lily sheen. I had never seen her look so lovely or, strangely enough, so serene. Serenity, in fact, was something I had never associated with her and it struck me some time later that it might well have been deliberately assumed, for the sole and irritating purpose of maddening Tina.

'Where are we going?' I said.

There was a gorgeous place about five miles up the river that a girl she knew had raved about : a place called Queen's Meadow. You could get there by bus. It seemed there was a boat-yard there and you could hire boats or canoes by the hour or the day. We would hire a boat, she thought, and row until we found some nice secluded spot where we could picnic and swim. Didn't I think it sounded better than Brighton?

I felt bound to agree that it did and half an hour later we were in the bus, riding up the flattish river valley, most of it flaming yellow with buttercups, with here and there a field cut newly for hay. It was already so hot that most of the windows of the bus were open and you could smell the glorious summer fragrance of hay as it poured in from across the river on the utterly tranquil morning air.

When it eventually came to hiring a boat from the big wooden boat-house at Queen's Meadow I had to confess that I didn't row very well. She gave me a tired sort of look about this and said she was rather beginning to despair of me.

'You don't swim. I hear you don't waltz. Now you can't row. What do you do?'

'I play a lot of tennis.'

'With some gorgeous creature, I suppose.'

'As a matter of fact she's plain and beefy. But she hits the ball like a man. I'm in a tournament with her next week.'

In slow and clumsy fashion I managed to row about half a mile up river, Sophie doing the steering. The water was very wide on that stretch of stream and it was too early for other boats to be out. This created an atmosphere of placidity that matched her own serenity to perfection and it was only after some time that I, in a moment of something like folly, suddenly broke it.

'What on earth was the matter with our Tina this morning?'

'She's growing up too fast.'

'Was that the cause of the grim glower? She didn't say a word.'

'She's got the tizzies about a man.'

'In love?'

'I suppose she thinks it is. She's threatened to run away. Or worse.'

For several moments I didn't say anything, but once again I was assailed by that trick of being haunted by one of the Davenports in absence; I saw once again Tina's dark-eyed face, contemptful, drained of gaiety; and finally said:

'And who is the victim? Or should it be the cause?'

'I wouldn't be a bit surprised if it's you.'

'Good God.'

'I'm afraid it is.'

'But hell! – it's ridiculous – she's so young –'

'What difference does that make?'

'Well, thank God I didn't give her any cause.'

'Cause? You promised to take her to a dance, didn't you?'

'Yes, but good God, that was merely to put her off.'

'You can't put our Tina off. She isn't the putting-off sort. No, she's deep in.'

A wave of irritation and wretchedness went through me. Suddenly I could see the morning, perhaps the entire day, in ruins. Stupidly I started thinking of how, sometimes, girls did demented things for love's sake or what they felt was love. The dark face of Tina again nagged and haunted me and then suddenly, in that typically disarming way of Sophie's, she was off at an airy tangent, waving an excited arm.

'Oh! look at all the water-lilies. Hundreds of them. Oh! this is the place. We must pull in here – pull in by the wood.'

From out of a dark reproachful cloud I passed, in less than half a minute, into sudden paradisical waters. I had never seen so many water-lilies: chalices of pure swan-white in great islands stretching half across the river, glittering in the perpendicular sun. A wood of mostly alders and poplars and fringed thick with reeds and many wild yellow flag irises stretched along one bank and I pulled the boat into it, marvelling at the wonder of it all, Tina forgotten.

After I had tied the boat up to a tree trunk and unloaded the picnic basket Sophie went into the wood to undress and change. A powerful impulse to follow her after some minutes and find her there in full nakedness went through me like white fire and I managed only to resist it because, all of a sudden, I felt that the morning had already lived too dangerously on complications.

She came out looking radiant. Her yellow swim-suit was as dazzling as her hair and I kissed her as she stood there in the sun. Her skin was beautifully warm as I touched it and all the serenity of the early day came back again.

The sight of her red head swimming about the waterlilies was like a fox moving among a flock of pure white birds. She swam with ease and grace, rather slowly, and once for more than a hundred yards upstream, calling as she came back that there were everywhere shoals of tiny fish. Then she lay flat on her back, almost motionless, floating, the air so supremely still all about her that I actually saw a grass snake swim across the river, leaving a thin trail of silver disturbance in its wake, head forked in the air.

I suppose she swam half a dozen times or more that morning and afternoon. In between her swims we lay sometimes in the sun and then, as the day grew hotter, in the thick alder shade. Mostly when I kissed her it was with the lazy somnolence of the day itself but once, in mid-afternoon, I drew down the shoulder straps of her swim-suit and put my mouth first against one breast and then the other and she stirred with ecstasy and said simply:

'You've been a long time coming to this.'

She had her last swim about eight o'clock. The air was still very warm but as she dived in I called after her that I would start to tidy up in readiness for going home. By now we had eaten every scrap of food and she called back that she was ravenously hungry and that we'd have to call at a pub somewhere and get a sandwich or a pie or she'd certainly die of it.

For a few minutes I stood watching her red head going downstream. Then I turned away to fetch her towel, which had been drying on a bush in the sun. The towel was warm and almost crisp to the touch as I picked it up and a moment later I bent down by the waterside and started to swill my face and hands.

When I stood upright again she had utterly disappeared. There was no sign anywhere of her flaming tiger head. My heart at once started thumping furiously and it seemed like a minute or more before my voice suddenly unlocked itself and I yelled her name.

'Sophie! For God's sake! Where are you? Sophie!'

For what seemed fully another minute there was no sign of her and no answer. I then started to run along the bank, downstream, desperate with fright, still calling her. I had a swift and awful vision of the ropes of water-lily roots strangling her down under the water and at last I stopped dead in my tracks, panting desperately and suddenly speechless and cold.

'Hullo there! What's all the noise?'

I turned with painful sharpness to see her fiery head and one arm waving clear above the water, thirty or forty yards back upstream. Sickly at first without a word I walked back towards her. She was laughing, her voice teasing and gay. I didn't know whether to laugh too or yell at her in anger and all I said was:

'Never do that to me again. God, I thought you'd gone –'

'Me? Never worry about me. I can take care of myself.'

She laughed gaily again and the tormenting sound of it once again woke in me that strange premonition I sometimes had about her, leaving a dark ghost behind.

I suppose it was half past ten or more before we got back to the café, having stopped to eat ham sandwiches at a pub on the way. The long hot day and much swimming had made her very tired and we didn't stop in the churchyard.

Much to my surprise the lights of the café were still on; but to my even greater surprise, when we went in, Mrs Davenport was standing tense-faced and white behind the counter, talking to a police sergeant named Baines, whom I had often had dealings with when on the paper. The sergeant was drinking a cup of tea and chewing slowly on a sausage roll.

'She's not back,' Mrs Davenport said. Her voice, more distant than usual, was chill and wooden. 'She's been gone since mid-day.'

Sergeant Baines swallowed a lump of sausage roll and looked rather hard at me and said:

'You haven't seen this young lady, I take it?'

'Not since morning.'

'Any idea where she might have gone? She spoke about dancing.'

I thought of the old manor house; then suddenly my dark premonition about Sophie transferred itself to Tina and I thought of the river. All of my fright about Sophie transferred itself to Tina too.

'I understand you went dancing with her sister last week. Where was that?'

'The old manor house.'

'Is there a dance there tonight?'

'I rather fancy so.'

'Oh! God, oh! God,' Mrs Davenport said and suddenly burst into tears, her face in her hands. Sophie immediately went behind the counter to comfort her. 'And you've been gone so long too. I thought you were never coming back.'

'Any more dances on tonight that you know of?'

'There's one at the Windmill Club.'

'I'll get down to the Manor House,' Sergeant Baines said. 'Would you nip across to the Windmill? You ought to find Constable Willis by the call-box at the corner of Charles Street and Denmark Avenue. It's nearly eleven. You know Willis, don't you? He'll probably come with you.'

The Windmill was about half a mile away and I ran most of the way. Curiously, and I suppose the sheer physical action may have been responsible, I hardly thought of Tina as I ran. I simply moved in a blind vacuum.

Constable Willis wasn't at the call-box but I met him half way up Denmark Avenue. After I had breathlessly tried to explain things he simply said, 'No need to run. No need to run,' and we walked on together in steady, police-like solemnity. It was then that my nerves really started to fret and sharply I said 'Where can the mad little fool have got to all this time?' to which Willis merely said:

'They don't often do nothing desperate.'

I then reminded him that he'd once before said something like that to me, on one of my routine visits to the station. That was the day Cathy Jacques had thrown herself out of a fifth-floor window of a factory.

'Yes, but very rare,' he said. 'Very rare.'

To the din of fox-trots and quick-steps I suppose we spent about half an hour looking about the Windmill dance floor. I had a word or two with several men I knew, but Tina clearly wasn't there. The strain of sheer desperation had now begun to make me feel in some way lost, almost light-headed, and at last I left and began to walk slowly back across the town.

By the time I got to the churchyard I began to feel as if someone had tied a steel knot across my brain. In sheer physical weariness I stopped for a few moments and leant by some iron railings and then, at last, slowly went on. Then as I passed the porch of the church something made me turn my head and look in and there she was, sitting on the stone seat like some damned God-forsaken penitent, her two hands in her lap.

In a situation both ludicrous and pathetic I hadn't even the strength to be angry with her or, for some time, to say a word. I was in no state either to reproach or inquire and at last I merely said:

'Come on. I'll take you back.'

For fully a minute she didn't say anything. Then I heard her give an enormous consuming sigh.

'Dance with me before we go.'

'I'm in no mood for dancing, thank you. Come on.'

She got to her feet, smoothing down her dress with her hands and then holding out her hands towards me.

'Just a dozen steps.'

I got up too and for half a minute danced with her about the stone floor of the porch. It was like dancing in a vault and my heart was cold.

Finally when I took her back into the café Sophie and her mother were taking a drop of the eternal comfort, a cup of tea. There was no fuss, no reproach, no recrimination. Mrs Davenport merely stared with those distant uninspired eyes of hers and passed sentence in five mysterious words whose meaning I wasn't fully to grasp for some long time:

'I've made up my mind.'

All the following week I kept away from the Davenports and instead played tennis with the plain beefy girl with the plain beefy name: Doris Plumpton. It wasn't until we had been knocked out of the semi-final of the tournament on the following Monday that I called round again at the little café, there to find the blinds, dark blue dusty ones, all drawn, and a notice on the window which read simply *These Premises to Let*.

So the Davenports, the golden lioness, the tiger-lily, the mischievous imp and Mrs Davenport, so often gay but sometimes not so gay, walked out of my life: as I thought, for ever.

It must have been five years later, perhaps nearer six, when on a fiery afternoon of Indian summer I was motoring across a stretch of chalk downland where a vast cathedral of beech trees smouldered vivid orange against a pale blue sky. Suddenly the day seemed altogether too good for motoring and I parked the car by a woodside and started walking instead. After about half an hour the beech-woods gave way to a gap in which lay a village with a squat-towered church of black-and-white flint, a few houses, a couple of shops, a pub called *The Fat Ox* and, at the far end of the street, a wayside café set in a biggish garden in which big banks of flowers still bloomed.

The afternoon was still warm and it suddenly struck me that a cold drink, perhaps a cup of tea, would be a good idea and I walked up to the café. The yellow-and-white hanging sign outside read *The Saffron Cake*, with another notice underneath *Closed*.

I stood for some moments incredulously bemused, slightly frustrated. Then I looked over the garden hedge. The garden stretched away quite large, laid out in enviable good order with big rose beds, lawns beautifully trimmed, great banks of dahlias, sunflowers and michaelmas daisies, and a pool with a white stone goddess in the centre of it, spilling a gentle fountain of water. Suddenly I caught sight of a woman sitting on a long blue-cushioned chair just beyond the pool, hatless, reading a book. It struck me at once that her hair might well have been a spray of autumn beech-leaves; it was almost, but not quite, that same splendid shade of orange red.

There was, I suddenly thought, no mistaking that hair. I opened the garden gate, walked across the lawn, beyond the pool and up to the blue-cushioned chair. As she heard my footsteps the woman in the chair sharply turned her head and gave a great start, staring at me with unbelievably bright brown eyes.

'Good God, it isn't Sophie.'

'Oh! my heavens you startled me.' She gave a puzzled sort of smile, at first uncertain and then of recognition. 'Oh! it can't be you. Where on earth have you sprung from?'

'I'm sorry I startled you. I was so sure it was Sophie.'

'No, it isn't Sophie. It's me.'

It was Mrs Davenport: a Mrs Davenport immensely, incredibly, miraculously changed, in fact transfigured. Her hair had been dyed not quite to that glorious tiger-lily shade of Sophie's, but almost; her lipstick matched it well; her two small pearl earrings and her plain pearl necklace, that might well have once been Christie's, were just right, suiting her perfectly. Her pale lime-green summer dress, with white collar and belt, gave her a remarkable freshness and in the same way so did her white pointed shoes. She might well, I thought, have been a fourth sister.

'But how ever did you find me? How did you know I was here?'

I said I didn't; it was just one of those things that happened sometimes.

'But you of all people to turn up. I still can't believe it. I've so often thought of you. I always meant to write.'

I said the garden was very beautiful and she said Yes, she had really spent a great deal of money on it since she'd come there two years before. At first she had been in the Chilterns but it was coldish there and she hadn't liked it much. Then she had seen this place advertised. It was a bit of a wreck at first but it had been fun, great fun, putting it right.

'It all seems to have been very successful.'

Oh! yes it had been very successful. She couldn't deny that. From the first the saffron cakes had gone with a bang. She now specialized in all sorts of other things too: cheese cakes, lard cakes, flead cakes, all manner of things, all from old recipes. She ran a mail order business. There was enough to keep four cooks busy and people came from far and near.

'I'm awfully glad. But I'm sorry you're closed.'

'Yes, I'm sorry about that too. But we always close on Wednesdays. It means we can open all day on Sundays. Sunday's the great day.'

I was getting ready to ask about the girls but she went on:

'Do sit down, won't you? No, not on the edge of the chair. It might tip up.' She threw me one of the blue cushions. 'Try that.'

So I sat on the blue cushion, on the grass, and then, still not quite recovered from my amazement at that transfiguration of hers, was about for the second time to ask about the girls when she said:

'Oh! yes it's turned out well. Really well.' She looked at me with warm directness, with eyes far removed from the uninspired distant gaze I had so often seen at the little café. 'I suppose I ought really to say thanks to you.'

'Me? Why me?'

'Don't you remember? That night you talked about inspiration?'

'Oh! that. I didn't think you took any notice of that.'

'Indeed I did.'

'But even then you didn't make up your mind.'

She suddenly gave the most engagingly mischievous smile,

so that for a second or two I saw all of Tina in her face, just as I had already seen much of Sophie in her hair.

'No, that didn't come until later. Until I realized I'd somehow got to put a stop to your tormenting my girls.'

I laughed aloud, hugely amused.

'Well, you don't deny it, do you? Making love to one one night and another the next. Dancing with Christie, swimming with Sophie. Driving young Tina up the wall.'

'I tormenting *them* ! And what,' I said, 'about their tormenting me?'

'I suppose so. They were really very beautiful, weren't they, say it as shouldn't?'

'Beautiful, my God? They were bewitching. If ever a man was led on.'

At that we both laughed together and in her voice I heard some of the old ringing gaiety of the girls.

'Yes, that was it. Inspiration and torment. And Davenport robbing the till every day. That was the last straw.'

Now, at last, I got in my question about the girls. Were the girls with her here?

'Oh ! the girls. No, they're not with me. I'm quite on my own. Christie married three years ago and emigrated to New Zealand. A young doctor. Tina's a shorthand typist. Works her way round the world. Taking a job here and a job there. Not married. She always was the independent one.'

She broke off and was silent for about a full minute, looking, I thought, rather pensive, with just a touch of the old distant air.

'And what,' I said, 'about Sophie?'

'It's getting a little chilly, don't you think? That's the worst of these October afternoons. As soon as the sun starts to go down. Would you care to see the rest of the garden?'

I said I would and she held out her right hand.

'Pull me up.'

Her hand was warm and smooth as I grasped it and I thought, instantly, of the warmth and smoothness of the girls. Then we started to walk across the garden and again I said :

'Tell me about Sophie. I always think I was somehow fondest of Sophie.'

We walked for some distance beyond big banks of scarlet dahlias, still untouched by frost, and massive golden clock-faces of sunflowers, before she answered.

'Sophie isn't with us any more.'

'No, good God, no.'

We walked the full length of the garden, not saying anything. My mind felt stunned with sorrow. What she was thinking I couldn't tell and at last she said:

'She was drowned one day last summer.'

'Great God, not Sophie. She could swim like an otter.'

'I sometimes think more swimmers are drowned than those who can't swim.'

'I'm terribly, terribly sorry.'

We came at last to a halt at a holly hedge at the farthest end of the garden and then stood looking at the great orange towers of beeches flaming above the naked chalk in the last shafts of afternoon sun. That flare of colour suddenly took me back to the afternoon when Sophie had swum about the water-lilies like a fox among a crowd of pure white birds. I remembered how I had kissed her breasts and how, for one terrible moment, I thought she had drowned.

For a minute or so I thought of telling Mrs Davenport about it and how, like a dark ghost, my premonition about Sophie had haunted me, but I couldn't bring myself to do it and suddenly she impulsively grasped my hand.

'Let's not think about it. It's one of my rules now never to go back into the past. Do you think that's wise?'

'It's probably wise.'

We started to walk back to the house. She was still grasping my hand and half way there she suddenly stopped and looked at me with a hint of affection in her bright brown eyes and said:

'It's very, very nice to see you. The girls were not the only ones in the family who always liked you. Shall we go in?'

'Yes, let's go in.'

She smiled. The air was growing cooler. I turned to catch, for a second or two, a final glimpse of the flaming, immemorial beeches.

'Good. It will,' she said, 'be much warmer inside.'

The Chords of Youth

'I WOULD absolutely stake my life,' my Aunt Leonora said, 'that it's Otto. The same, same old Otto. Even after thirty years I'd know that marvellous forehead anywhere. That fine brow.'

With a rising shrillness in her voice, never in any case an instrument much subdued, she brandished a copy of the *Flimshurst Courier & Gazette* in front of my face with all the excited ardour of a messenger arriving with news of some positive and splendid victory.

'Look at that face. Look at it. Wouldn't you know it anywhere?'

With what I hoped was pointed if casual gentleness I reminded my Aunt Leonora that I had never met Otto. I had never, until that moment, even heard of Otto. Otto, for all I knew or could guess, might never have existed. He was yet another of those figures out of the vast social mythology that, over the years, Aunt Leonora conjured up so smoothly and sweetly to amuse herself and deceive and infuriate the rest of us. Otto, without doubt, belonged to those picnics she thought had been arranged but hadn't, those couples she thought were in love but weren't, to all those various misguided and tangled lives she thought ought to be re-moulded nearer to her particular heart's desire simply in order to give her the serene satisfaction of feeling that their new-shaped destinies were her own.

'We met,' she suddenly said with that inconsequent entanglement of near-truth and near-falsehood, not quite downright lying, that formed the greater part of her charm, 'in Switzerland. We climbed the Zugspitze together.'

'The Zugspitze happens,' I said, 'to be in Germany.'

'Well, wherever it was. I know it was somewhere near the frontier.'

'The nearest frontier to the Zugspitze,' I pointed out, 'is Austria.'

'Very well, Austria then. I know it was somewhere there. Why on earth do you always have to split hairs?'

I was about to point out, with all the blandness in the world, that there were times when some degree of accuracy helped, one way or another, when she smartly brandished the copy of *The Courier & Gazette* at me a second time. Didn't I agree that it was Otto? That it couldn't possibly be anyone else but Otto?

'You see,' she said, now baring her long teeth in one of those maddeningly disarming smiles of hers, 'it's so typical. I mean this twinning of towns idea. Adopting one another, one English and one German. He was all for that sort of thing, fraternity and so on. Aren't you? You've heard of it, haven't you?'

One moment she was flashing her golden spectacles at me in insistent demand for an answer; the next she was wheeling round with affectionate vehemence on my Uncle Freddie, who was sitting with sublime comfort in his easy chair, sopping a slice of buttered toast in his tea.

'I –' Freddie said. 'What? –'.

'That was Otto all over,' she said. 'That's how we all were at the Hirschen. The Gasthof. At six o'clock in the evening none of us knew each other – German, Swiss, English, Austrian, total strangers, the lot – by midnight we were all in love. Next day we were all haring up the Zugspitze.'

A gift for exaggeration is not the least of my Aunt Leonora's charms. A sudden monstrous turn of phrase will serve to extinguish, as if by magic, all her tiresome, fibbing garrulity. In consequence, I loved the sentence 'haring up the Zugspitze'. It endeared her so much to you that you forgave her all tedium, all chatter. It even made me smile.

'I can't think what there is to smile at,' she said, 'and keep those eyes of yours to yourself. They're always wandering.' She gave me one of those dark accusatory glares of hers, at the same time half-hinting that I was somehow corrupting Freddie. 'It's no use looking at Freddie, either. He's all for it, too.'

All for what I didn't know and had no time to ask before she went on, with an almost blithe shrillness of joy:

'That's the thing that makes me so sure it is Otto. It's so exactly like him. He'd have everybody blood-brothers in no time. I mean anybody, no matter. For instance this exchange of towns idea. The mayor of this in Germany and the mayor of that in England. Just like him. I think we really ought to try to love the Germans, don't you?'

'No.'

'What do you mean? – no?'

'No.'

In a withering second she turned cold on me; her spectacles were icy.

'No? I'm shocked. I thought you were so frightfully keen on that sort of thing?'

'What sort of thing?'

'International good-will and all that. International under-standing. You're always on about it, anyway. It's one of your hobby-horses.'

It was a typical, blatant, outrageous lie. I will admit, it is true, to a few hobby-horses, but international good-will is not one of them. I am, on the whole, less interested in that subject than in the love-making of snails. It was now my turn to be icy.

'And that, I suppose, is a picture of the great Otto you've got there?'

She snapped *The Courier & Gazette* at me with all the crack-ling vehemence of a pistol trigger being cocked.

'I don't know what's behind that word great,' she said, 'but there isn't a doubt that's him, being greeted by the Mayor of Flimshurst at the quayside.'

'Not the mayor. The Chairman of the Urban District Council.'

'Well, whatever he is. Anyway, I think he ought to be Mayor. It sounds so much more equal.'

Eagerly but coldly watched by Aunt Leonora, I turned to the picture, on the front page of *The Courier & Gazette*, of Anglo-German friendship. The Chairman of the Urban District Coun-cil looked, except for a thick ecclesiastical bunch of white hair curling in his neck, remarkably like a well-gnawed bone. He also looked to me like the kind of man who smiles too easily. A glittering chain of office was looped about his neck.

In his left hand he was holding aloft the German flag; with his right he was shaking hands in smiling effusion with a bald-headed man whose face looked like a pot of lard that has boiled over and eventually congealed in white, flabby, unhealthy drifts and folds. He was waving the Union Jack. Enthusiastic and even strenuous though this gesture was, he somehow hardly looked to me like a man who had ever, even in youth, scaled high mountains. Nor could I detect in the heavy Teutonic furrows of his face any sign of that marvellous forehead, that fine brow.

'And what,' I said, 'did you say that Otto's other name was?'

'Oh! Heimberger. Hunnegar. Honnegger. Heimburg. Something like that.'

'According to the paper here this is a Herr Otto Untermeyer.'

'Oh! is it? Oh! yes, I suppose it could be. After all these years. Untermeyer – well, yes, it isn't all that – anyway, it does say Otto?'

'It does say Otto.'

'Good, then it must be. It positively couldn't be anyone else.'

Here I thought it pertinent to ask:

'Yes, but does it look anything like the man? Would you recognize him again, for instance?'

'I shall invite him to tea. No, lunch. That would give us more time.' She actually laughed as she suddenly stopped talking of lunch and scaled the inconsequent steps of memory. 'The thing I remember most is the wild flowers. Gentians and soldanellas and anemones – those lovely big greyish-yellow ones. And the butterflies. And the vast amounts of sausage. *Wurst – Liberwurst, Bratwurst* – Oh! it became quite a joke, the *wurst*. Especially with Otto. Follow me, all, he would say – *Achtung!* all will now follow – *Achtung!* – I will go *wurst! Wurst*, you see? – first!'

I said I saw; Uncle Freddie, at the same moment, rather dismally started to sop the last piece of buttered toast in his tea.

Abruptly and unexpectedly, as she often did, Aunt Leonora became pensive. Behind the dancing golden spectacles, so icy a few minutes before, her eyes became dreamy, wide and globular. She might for a second or two have been living again some long-uncaptured moment of Teutonic romance, gentian-starred, listening to a thousand-belled peal of soldanellas between summer meadows and summer snow – or that, at least, is what I thought until with equal abruptness all her dreaminess evaporated and she said with that simplicity that both endeared and disarmed:

'I should like to show him something really English. A real English memory. Like the *wurst* is for me. As German as that is, only English. You know?'

I was about to say I didn't know and then to make some innocent suggestion about fish-and-chips when she suddenly gave a series of chirps, either of delight or revelation or both, and danced across the room to pick up the telephone directory.

'Oh! what is his name, that man, that Chairman of the Council fellow? I know it as well as my own. Doesn't he keep a shop or something?'

'Several. Among other things.'

'Other things? What other things?'

'Anything that will earn a dishonest penny.'

She glowered at me with extreme accusation.

'I always thought you judged people too hastily,' she said. 'There's good in everybody.'

I said I didn't doubt it; you had to be good to go as far as her George Wilbram, Chairman of the Urban Council, had done.

'What was that? What did you say? Don't mumble so. I'm always telling you.'

'You'll find him under Wilbram,' I said. 'Or Augustine Developments or Abbey Enterprises.'

'What charming names. I think I'll try Augustine. Will you come to lunch too? I think you'd adore Otto. Something tells me you'd have a great deal in common.'

While waiting for Mr Wilbram's number to come through

she several times urged me to put my thinking-cap on in the matter of German wines. We had to do our utmost to do Otto well on that score; we had to match the vintage to the guest.

'Rather *soignée*,' she said. 'You know what I mean? I don't know the German word. There must be one, mustn't there?'

I started to say that undoubtedly there must and turned in readiness to wink at Uncle Freddie, only to find that he had dropped off, head on chest, the last piece of buttered toast precariously poised in his fingers, like some half-smoked cigar.

'Oh! Mr Wilbram? You won't know me, but – I saw all about that marvellous Anglo-German unity thing of yours. Yes. In the paper. Oh! yes, I'm a great friend of Otto. We once climbed together.'

Ten minutes later, after a conversation as one-sided as the progress of a snow-fed torrent careering down one of the many valleys at the foot of the Zugspitze, Aunt Leonora at last drew breath, went in brief silence to the window and looked across, eastward and southward, to the modest summer hills that grace the skyline like folds of gentlest green cloth between her house and the sea.

In the sigh that she finally and suddenly gave there was, I thought, a depth not unmystical. It revealed too, like her words, how tender and endearing at heart she really was.

'If we can't show him gentians and anemones and soldanellas and all that we can at least show him the orchids. All those rare native ones of ours that grow up there – the Spider, the Butterfly, the Bee, the Soldier – you know – they're so English, aren't they? And to think that the Romans must have seen them too – marvellous thought!'

She actually gave a short, ecstatic clap of her hands. Much startled, Uncle Freddie woke with a jump. The remaining piece of buttered toast dropped into his tea-cup. With feverish haste he scrambled to his feet, knocking cup into saucer, looking rather like a pink, fat baby roused cruelly from milky slumber, and said:

'What was that? I thought you called me.'

'The most marvellous thing has happened,' she said. 'A sort

77

of Prodigal Son thing – in a way, sort of.' She suddenly turned to me those inquisitive innocent spectacles of hers, as if seeking some confirmation of this preposterous parallel of hers. 'Don't you think so? It *is* rather like that, don't you feel? – Otto coming back. Quite a miracle in a way. Don't you think so?'

'No.'

'Oh?' For a single second she looked wildly hurt. Then she looked utterly stern. 'And if it isn't a miracle what in your precious book is it then?'

Something prompted me to say 'the trump of doom', but I remembered myself in time and said:

'Never mind about the miracles. What are you going to give them to eat? I'd like the wine and the food to marry as well as they can.'

'Steak and kidney pudding,' she said with such promptitude that Uncle Freddie actually emerged into full consciousness, like a schoolboy bidden to a sudden banquet. 'And Christmas pudding for afters. I always keep one or two back – one for Easter and one for emergencies.'

Uncle Freddie actually gave something like a cheer. 'The old Kate and Sidney!' he started to say when she abruptly interrupted him with renewed sternness, as if rebuking the man for interrupting holy ritual.

'That will do,' she said and suddenly rose inconsequently away from both of us and such worldly matters as steak and kidney pudding by saying very softly, in a sentence now more mysterious than mystical: 'I'd have you know the chords of youth are sometimes very slender,' leaving us both abruptly chastened and without an answer.

It was only some long time later that it occurred to me that the word might well have been 'tender'.

For lunch on the following Friday I selected a white wine, a *Deidesheimer Hofstück* '59. That this was unlikely to marry very well with the steak and kidney pudding, or for that matter with the Christmas pudding either, was something that hardly seemed to matter. Nothing else would marry anyway. The choice was merely a gesture in the cause of Anglo-German unity. With the *Deidesheimer Hofstück* '59 we made our bow, so to speak, to the Reich. With the two puddings we raised the English standard high.

For some time before lunch I had an uneasy feeling that Aunt Leonora might take the cause of friendship even further. For some reason or other I was over-possessed by the notion that the chords of youth might well prompt her to go, ridiculous though it may sound, all Bavarian, peasant costume and all. I need hardly have worried. She finally appeared in a mustard-and-pepper tweed costume, a shirt blouse and brown brogue shoes.

These, she said, were just the stuff for walking.

'Oh! Herr Untermeyer. Otto. It was weather just like this, wasn't it? You remember? A little mist first thing and then – *achtung!* the sun. *Wurst!*'

Herr Untermeyer looked much more than startled. I could have sworn that his transparent pork-like eyes, too small for the immense inflated paper-bag of his face, turned pink. He looked, gross and flabby in a grey summer suit cut to disguise the vast lines of his figure and now much-creased with travelling, very like a prisoner rudely captured on a foreign field, nervously wondering if his captors were about to treat him well or not.

'Wasn't this a piece of luck, Mr Wilbram? It was just by chance that I saw it in the paper. What's the name of the town you're twinning with, or adopting, or whatever it is?'

'Traben. It's –'

'Oh! would that be near the Zugspitze? Have you been to that part, Mr Wilbram? There's a marvellous blue lake there. All blue.'

'No, I haven't,' Mr Wilbram said. 'It's farther north – Traben, I mean.'

'You've talked to Otto about how we met and climbed the Zugspitze and all that, I suppose? It's all of thirty years.'

'Herr Untermeyer doesn't speak English very easily,' Mr Wilbram said. 'He's all right if he takes it slowly.'

'Really? It used to be so beautiful.'

'Yes? I suppose you tend to forget it over the years.'

Mr Wilbram might, I thought, have been a medieval prelate. His lean countenance – face is too simple a word – exuded goodness as a ripe plum exudes juice, except that there was neither juice nor ripeness in Mr Wilbram. The goodness of his eye was cold. His hair, white and slightly curled as fresh lamb's wool, as I had noted in the picture in the newspaper, had been allowed to grow rather long in his neck, where you felt it had been carefully tended with a comb of piety.

'Now what about a drink? You,' she said to me, 'organize the drinks with Freddie. A pink gin for me. And you, Mr Wilbram, what for you?'

'For me, nothing. I rarely –'

'No? Not even for an occasion – a day like this?'

'For an occasion, sometimes. But midday, never.'

'But Otto will. Herr Untermeyer? You'll have a little – *schniff*, you know? You remember *schniff*? You remember how we all used to have *schniffs*? I said in English we called it snifter and you said in German it was *schnapps* and so in the end it got to *schniffs*. Eh? You remember? That was a good example of Anglo-German unity all right, Mr Wilbram, wasn't it? *Schniffs*?'

'I suppose it was,' Mr Wilbram said.

'And that,' she said, 'in the early days of the Nasties too. I always called them the Nasties. So much nearer the truth. Still, we'll forget all that. Enough of that. This is *our* day, isn't it, Otto? What about a *schniff* now?'

Herr Untermeyer, it seemed to me, didn't seem to think it was their day. Nor, I thought, was he much inclined to *schniffs*. Prisoner-like still, he stood painfully erect, as if under orders of silence, awaiting the terms of his sentence.

'I know! I'll give him red-currant wine,' she said. 'After all it was in Germany I first drank it. And you, Mr Wilbram, too? Yes? It's my own – from a German recipe. *Guht*, yes? Red-currant, Otto, you understand? That will do you?'

'So,' Herr Untermeyer said.

'Your pink gin,' I said, 'or would you rather have red-currant now?'

'Oh! red-currant, I think, now, don't you? I think so. It's all the better for the unity.'

So we drank red-currant for unity. Even Mr Wilbram drank a modest half-glass, sipping it with something between a touch of disapprobation and an air of penance, rather as if it were communion wine. By contrast Herr Untermeyer seemed to approve greatly. Uncle Freddie had somehow drawn him aside, towards the window, through which and over ruby glasses they were contemplating the hills.

'Orchids,' I heard Uncle Freddie say. 'Very rare.' Uncle Freddie raised his glass, in what might have been a gesture of salutation. 'You know them? Orchids? They are disappearing fast.'

'*So?* Disappearing?'

'My wife,' Uncle Freddie said, making another gesture with his glass towards the hills, 'will show them to you. After lunch. Up there. You like the wine?'

'Was good.'

'I'm rather for it myself,' Uncle Freddie said and reached out to a side-table for the bottle. In re-filling Herr Untermeyer's glass and his own he referred once or twice more to the orchids. It was a great shame. They were disappearing fast. A tragedy. Being stolen, he explained. It was the same in Germany, he supposed? Picnickers and motorists and all that? –'

'The rape of the countryside,' Aunt Leonora said. 'Oh! I'm sure it goes on everywhere. That at least we have in common.'

'In common? Rape?' Herr Untermeyer stared at Aunt Leonora greatly mystified, eyes rapidly growing pinker. 'So? This word I am not knowing. And orchids? *Was* is orchids?'

'They are referring,' Mr Wilbram said, 'to a certain kind of flower. *Blumen.*'

'Ah! *blumen.* So?'

'Some,' Aunt Leonora said, 'are shaped like soldiers. And some like spiders. And some like men.'

'Soldiers?' Herr Untermeyer said. '*Blumen?* This I am not –'

'Soldiers,' Aunt Leonora said. 'What is the German for soldiers? *Wehrmacht?*'

'No, no. *Soldaten*,' Mr Wilbram said. '*Soldaten*.'

'We have them shaped like butterflies too,' Uncle Freddie said. 'And bees. And there is one, the *Military* –'

'*Soldaten*? Ah! you are in military service?'

'Do I smell something boiling over?' I said.

Aunt Leonora promptly rushed to the kitchen, calling as she went, 'Don't rush, don't rush. We'll be ten minutes yet. Give everybody another *schniff*, dear boy, will you? Don't let Otto get dry.'

I immediately armed myself with a fresh bottle of red-currant.

'Another *schniff*, Herr Untermeyer?'

'*Danke. Schniff*? What is this word *schniff*?'

I was about to say that it was a word born out of international fraternity or something of that sort when Mr Wilbram said:

'From here, Herr Untermeyer, we are actually looking straight across to where the Romans camped. Straight up there.'

Herr Untermeyer, glass replenished, eyes pinker than ever, slowly followed the direction of Mr Wilbram's pointing finger to the line of hills a mile or two away.

'Takes you back a bit, doesn't it?' Uncle Freddie said. 'Always gives me a sense of history. To think the Romans –'

'Romans?' Herr Untermeyer said. His eyes were fixed on the hills in a kind of jellified mystification. 'Romans?'

'Ceasar's soldiers,' Mr Wilbram said. '*Soldaten – Romanisch* –'

'*Ja, ja*!' Herr Untermeyer said. '*So*! I understood.' All mystification gone, all military secrets unravelled, Herr Untermeyer actually laughed, bellying guffaws, begging us please to excuse the badness of his understanding about the *blumen*. He had foolishly confused them with the military. *Blumen* were for gardens, *ja*?

'You do much climbing now?' Uncle Freddie said.

What answer Herr Untermeyer was about to give to this discomforting question I never knew. In that same moment Aunt Leonora came back from the kitchen, instantly seized Herr Untermeyer affectionately by the arm and led him to the window. For an awful moment or two I saw us being launched yet again on the tortuous seas of flora and fauna, of orchids and Romans, *blumen* and the military, when to my infinite surprise she looked Otto straight in the face and said:

'Let's have a good look at you. No. You really haven't changed. Not all that much. I'd have known you again – even without the photograph.' In a gesture of affection quite touching in its disarming simplicity she held up her pink gin. '*Schniff*, eh, Otto? Cheers! *Wurst*! It's such a pleasure to have you here.'

'Also for me it is great pleasure. Also to be in England.'

'Herr Untermeyer loves England,' Mr Wilbram said. 'Except for the sausages, eh, Herr Untermeyer!' Mr Wilbram gave a brief, harsh crackle of a laugh. 'Not the sausages.'

'Not the sausages?' Aunt Leonora said. 'No? Not the *wurst*?'

'He thinks they are very bad,' Mr Wilbram said. 'Very bad.'

'Bad. Bad. Very bad,' Otto said. 'Most bad. Most.'

'Good God, what's wrong with them?' Uncle Freddie said. 'I get raring hungry at the thought of them. When can we eat, dear?'

'Bad, the sausage, very bad. The *wurst*, in England, very bad. They are not ripe.'

'Ah, ah! We have had this before,' Mr Wilbram said. 'By ripe – I should explain – he means they have no flavour.'

'They have not the strong!' Herr Untermeyer said, suddenly making gestures of powerful vehemence with his clenched massive lardy fists, so that for a moment or two Aunt Leonora recoiled, positively alarmed. 'They have not the force! You understood?'

'The melons,' my Aunt Leonora suddenly said, in one of those typically inconsequent moments of hers that both charm and dismay, 'weren't quite as ripe as I should have liked them – they're a little bit tricky as late as this in August. So we have to begin without them, I'm afraid.' With those long, disengaging teeth of hers she flashed at each of us in turn, a separate disarming smile. 'Aren't I lucky? Four men. Shall we go in before everything gets cold?'

'Praise the Lord and pass the ammunition!' Uncle Freddie said. 'The good old Kate and Sidney.'

There were always moments when Uncle Freddie, fired by an extra glass or two of something, particularly red-currant wine, was liable to become harmlessly jocular, but now I thought I detected in the cold goodness of Mr Wilbram's eye an answering glint of disquiet, as if Freddie had been guilty of a spasm of blasphemy.

Undeterred, ripe-faced and famished, Freddie stood at the head of the lunch table. brandishing a knife and fork over the steak and kidney pudding like a priest preparing a sacrifice.

'Nothing like the good old Kate and Sidney!'

'Kate and Sidney?' Mr Wilbram said, his cold good eyes fixed on the puffed white crust of the pudding, large as a football, his voice again frosty, as if once more a slight blasphemy had been committed.

'*Gate und* –'

Herr Untermeyer too looked confused, pink, questioning eyes on the pudding, from the crust of which Uncle Freddie now proceeded to cut a generous slice, so that steam rose forth.

'I never heard it called this before,' Mr Wilbram said, rather as if he had just heard that some alien clause had been introduced into the *Sermon on the Mount*. ' "Kate and Sidney" –?'

'It's a kind of joke,' I said.

'Rhyming slang,' Uncle Freddie said. 'By God, the crust's beautiful. Apples and pears. Trouble and strife. Tit for tat. Plates, please, plates. Where are the plates?'

'Right in front of your eyes, dear.'

'We have this special kind of slang,' I started to explain to Herr Untermeyer, who looked increasingly bewildered. 'Tit for tat: hat. So you get titfer. It's a joke – a *scherz*,' I said, this being the only German word I could think of that meant light. 'A joke-*scherz*,' I repeated several times. 'You see?'

Herr Untermeyer, who had been standing at attention all this time, said he did not understood.

'Oh! do please sit down, everybody,' Aunt Leonora said. 'And stop prattling,' – this to me, quite sharply, as if I had been guilty of more or less continued flippancy. 'The wine is far more important. Show Otto the wine.'

'*Wasser, bitte*,' Herr Untermeyer started to say and for one uneasy moment I thought that the carefully chosen *Deidesheimer Hofstück* '59 might after all go unappreciated. 'Pliss may I –'

'Oh! yes, I'm sorry,' Mr Wilbram said. 'It's my fault. Herr Untermeyer has to have a glass of water. He has tablets to take.'

'For the hard.' Herr Untermeyer tapped his chest several times. 'Also when the bad wind is blowing. From the East –'

'I'll go, I'll go,' Aunt Leonora said and then as suddenly gave the water-fetching task to me. 'You go. I must hand the vegetables. We have no help, Otto, you see.'

When I got back to the lunch table again, a glass of water in one hand and a bottle of the *Deidesheimer Hofstück* '59 in the other, Herr Untermeyer had a private array of bottles set out in front of him, one containing green pills, one pink and two white.

I set the glass of water in front of him and at the same time prepared to show him the *Deidesheimer Hofstück* '59. A rich and seductive odour of meat pudding filled the air. Assailed by this, by the sight of the wine-bottle and by the enforced necessity of pill-taking, Herr Untermeyer sat in further confusion, painfully beset by the opposing forces of denial and indulgence, his large frame breathing heavily.

'I hope you will like the wine, Herr Untermeyer,' I said and to my relief he turned on the bottle with a gesture of hardly concealed joy, actually caressing it with his fat fingers. 'Ah! is *guht*. Is very nice. From my part of Germany. You understood?'

In the same moment Aunt Leonora set in front of him a plate generously heaped with pudding, mashed potatoes flecked with parsley butter, French beans and cauliflower, the whole caressed by the rich dark gravy of the Kate and Sidney.

As Herr Untermeyer gazed down on this with an almost tortured expression of pleasure and anticipation I heard Mr Wilbram plead with Aunt Leonora in a whisper almost deathly:

'A mere half of that for me, Mrs Elphinstone. A mere half. Less if possible. Even less. I am not a great eater.'

As Mr Wilbram's frame bore a sharp resemblance to one of

those pallid marble effigies, horizontally embalmed for ever in stony piety, that one sees in churches, it was impossible to imagine that he ever ate much at all, except perhaps toast and dry cornflakes.

'Would you please try the wine, Herr Untermeyer?' I said.

'You know you're not really supposed to, Otto,' Mr Wilbram said.

'Ah? You say?'

'*Verboten*, Otto,' Mr Wilbram said. '*Verboten.*'

'*Mit* the pills, yes, yes. I can do. Is all right.'

'No, no. *Verboten*. Remember now. You told me yourself. One glass and then *verboten*.'

'No, no! *Mit* the pills,' Herr Untermeyer said, 'is *guht*. Is all right.'

Mr Wilbram shook his head with a gesture of sad goodness, gloomily exhorting Herr Untermeyer to remember that after all it was he, not Mr Wilbram, who would suffer.

In answer Herr Untermeyer suddenly tasted the wine with a positive gasp of pleasure.

'*Wunderbar!*'

'Well, well, have it your way,' Mr Wilbram said. The tone of his voice was that of one icily delivering judgement.

'Don't say I didn't warn you. You remember the attack in Traben last year?'

'That,' Herr Untermeyer said, 'was not the same. Was different on that occasion. Was then the *lieber*. Now, *mit* the pills, the *lieber* is *guht*. The *wein* I can in little bits take now.'

'All right, all right. It's on your head,' Mr Wilbram said. 'It's on your head.'

'Oh! come, a little wine after all,' Aunt Leonora said, 'for thy stomach's sake. It maketh glad the heart of man, surely. And anyway this is something of an occasion. Nothing like wine for warming up the international fellowship, is there? We saw that at the Hirschen, didn't we, Otto?'

'I'll bet it wasn't backward in flowing forward at Traben last year either,' Uncle Freddie said. 'By God, the Kate and Sidney's good. Sorry if I've started.'

'Oh! yes, do start, Otto,' Aunt Leonora said. 'Please don't let it get cold.'

Herr Untermeyer at once struck into the steak and kidney pudding with the enthusiasm of a man long deprived of nourishment. The pills stood before him forgotten. The gross nature of his pleasure was now and then reflected in monosyllables richly content and sometimes, unlike the English sausage, ripe. '*Schön!*' was one of these and '*Budding*' another.

'How you call this *budding* again? A *joke?*' Herr Untermeyer turned on from the depths of his stomach a positive diapason of voluptuous approval and pleasure. 'This is not *joke*. This is *himmel!* *Was* is this flesh?' he said, holding up a succulent square of steak speared at the end of his fork. 'How is this called?'

'Not flesh,' Mr Wilbram said. 'Meat. Steak.'

'To rhyme with Kate,' Uncle Freddie said.

'How is this. Ah! this you call it? Kate? How you say like that? Kate?'

'No, steak,' Mr Wilbram said. 'Steak. Kate is a figure of speech. So to speak.'

'So? *Kate budding*, so? This I love. This is *himmel*, Frau Elphinstein, *himmel*. My bestest congratulations on your kitchen. *Danke*. I give you *Schniff!*'

'*Schniff!*' Aunt Leonora said. '*Schniff!* Oh! how that word takes me back.'

'The chords of youth,' I said and raised my glass of *Deidesheimer Hofstück* '59.

'What was that?' she said sharply. 'I've told you before. Don't mumble so.'

'I was simply praising the pudding.'

'Oh! were you? All I can say is it sounded a funny sort of praise.'

If my own praise was odd and whispered, that of Herr Untermeyer continued to be splendidly articulate. Between gargantuan mouthfuls of meat and vegetable and crust he hardly paused for breath. Nor, for a man who wasn't a very great eater, did Mr Wilbram, I thought, appear to be doing badly either. Spots of gravy actually dribbled down the front of his shirt as he pushed his loaded fork into his mouth. Only now and then, as if some force in him slightly disapproved of the enjoyments of the flesh, did he suddenly desist, glance genially at Aunt Leonora as if in fear that his plate might be empty before that of Otto, and then forge on again.

He need have had no qualms about the plates; Otto's was white and clean while Mr Wilbram was still mopping up the last forkfuls of kidney and potato.

'Now, now, come along, everybody. I want none of it left. More for you, Otto? Yes!'

'*Schön! Schön! Schön* beyond speak. No? That is not right?'

'What is right then? Unspeak? – unspeakable?'

Uncle Freddie and I laughed aloud and Aunt Leonora, beaming with those long, impossible white teeth of hers, said:

'Oh! you're quite a dear, Otto. You're really a great dear. You don't change a scrap. Give Otto more wine. And I won't say "No" either.'

'Better open another bottle, dear boy,' Uncle Freddie said. 'That's if there *is* a second?'

'And a third,' I said.

'Good show. There's a certain something about this German wine.'

'Oh! we drank oceans of it at the Hirschen, didn't we, Otto? Positive oceans.'

'*Wein* we may have in Germany. *Guht wein*. Much *wein*. But not this *budding*. No.'

Soon, I noticed, even Mr Wilbram was enjoying that certain something in the German wine. Its influence rose about the lunch table like a breath of flowers. We *schniffed* exhaustively. Aunt Laura *schniffed* to the Zugspitze and Herr Untermeyer, actually standing up, glass upraised, *schniffed* to England, and to my great surprise, 'the gliffs of Dover'. This gliffs of Dover had, it seemed, moved him immeasurably.

'From the sea, from the ship, I am seeing this gliffs. So white. They are so *schön* and white and I am weeping.'

'May I in return,' Mr Wilbram said, 'pledge our faith in Germany? Perhaps I ought to say the new Germany?'

'I think you'd better,' Aunt Leonora said, in one of those charmingly swift diplomatic thrusts of hers that are always over before you can do anything about them. 'To hell with the old. I mean the Nasties. You know what I mean.'

'That,' Mr Wilbram said, 'is what we are all trying to forget.'

'You may be,' she said, 'but not me.'

On this very slightly discordant note she got up from the table and started to clear the dishes, urging us all at the same time to stay where we were, and then presently went off to the kitchen, whispering as she passed me:

'Brandy or rum, do you think?'

'Rum,' I said. 'It burns better.'

As we waited for her return I drained the second bottle of *Deidesheimer Hofstück* '59. This led Uncle Freddie to praise it, not for the first time, as a wine that one could drink a good deal of and not feel the difference.

Herr Untermeyer strongly agreed. 'That is so. You are not feeling it. Not in the head. Not in the legs. Only in the hard. How do you say this? – this *wein* is like – how are you saying? – a *lieder*? –'

'A song.'

'A song, *jawohl*. That is so. A song. A song for the hard.'

'Brings back the good old days, I'll bet,' Uncle Freddie said. 'Slopes of the Zugspitze and all that. I often wonder what you got up to on that mountain.'

'International fellowship,' I said.

Any glint of remonstrance in Mr Wilbram's eye was promptly extinguished by the entrance of Aunt Leonora, bringing the Christmas pudding, bearing it aloft like some blue-flamed dark head on a charger.

'My God, she's well alight,' Uncle Freddie said.

'It's the rum,' I said. 'Far better than brandy.'

'Let's have a drop more on, dear boy,' Freddie said. 'Don't let her die down. Splendid show.'

As Aunt Leonora finally bore the flaming pudding to the

table Uncle Freddie and I raised an appropriate cheer. Herr Untermeyer, pink eyes transfixed by this newly offered sacrifice, actually clapped his fat hands, delighted as a child at the rum-fed flames.

'Looks marvellous,' Uncle Freddie said.

'I only hope it will be good,' Aunt Leonora said. 'I always think they taste better for keeping. Don't you think so, Mr Wilbram? Does your wife keep yours?'

Mr Wilbram said he rather thought not. They were rarely at home for Christmas. He suddenly ran his finger round his shirt collar, looking flushed and discomforted. Wasn't it rather warm, didn't we think? Would anyone mind if we opened a window?

It was rather warm, Aunt Leonora suddenly confessed, and while Uncle Freddie was feeding the expiring flames on the pudding with more rum I went to the window and opened it, surprised to see how the day had flowered from an early morning fogginess, clothed in softest white cloud, to a blazing afternoon. The hills shone golden with a purity of light that only the marriage of sea and late summer could give.

'Perfect afternoon,' I said. 'Splendid for walking.'

Uncle Freddie gave me a sharpish sort of look, which I ignored, and Aunt Leonora said while I was up would I hand her the cream? As I picked up the cream-boat from the sideboard I heard Mr Wilbram say:

'I don't want to put a damper on things, Mrs Elphinstone, but I feel I ought to say that Herr Untermeyer has an engagement at five. He's christening a bus.'

'Good God, man,' she said, 'since when have buses had to be christened?'

'It's a joint Anglo-German effort,' Mr Wilbram said. 'The two towns have shared the cost, Traben and ours. It's for the old people. Excursions and so on. It's going to be called *The Lorelei*. It's Herr Untermeyer's idea.'

'The chords of youth again,' I said.

'What did you say?' Mr Wilbram said, 'I didn't quite catch that.'

'Oh! take no notice,' Aunt Leonora said. 'In any case there's plenty of time for the bus. It isn't two o'clock yet. You'll want to walk your lunch down, won't you?'

Mr Wilbram, I thought, didn't look at all as if he wanted to walk his lunch down.

'Ah! the fire is now out,' Herr Untermeyer said, rubbing his hands.

'Drop more rum do you think?' Uncle Freddie said and was about to feed the dying flames a second time when Aunt Leonora waved him aside and started to cut generous wedges of Christmas pudding, at the same time saying to Herr Untermeyer:

'Now, Otto, you'll taste this? Something very specially English. They don't even have it in Scotland.' What this had to do with it I simply couldn't think. 'I'm sorry there aren't any good-luck charms. But then we're grown-up, aren't we?'

'This also is a *budding*?'

'Yes, but for Christmas.'

'Ah! so? But Christmas it is not now. It is now summer.'

'Yes, but we saved it from last year.'

The expression on Herr Untermeyer's face clouded from mere bewilderment to fogged mystification. The Christmas pudding steamed with richness. Aunt Leonora drowned a mountainous wedge of it in cream, Uncle Freddie topped up the wine glasses and Mr Wilbram further complicated things by saying:

'I suppose it's something left over from pre-Christian times. I mean the dried fruit and all that. The feast of the Winter Solstice and so on. Very little for me, Mrs Elphinstone, please, very little. I've really had an excellent sufficiency.'

'I admit it does blow you up a bit,' Uncle Freddie said.

'Winter?' Herr Untermeyer said. 'Winter? Why you now say winter?'

'Oh! you'll soon walk that off,' Aunt Leonora said and carved Mr Wilbram a slice of pudding, darkly rich and steaming, as generous as Otto's, topping it with cream. 'Anyway you can always run down the hills. If not up them.'

With dismay Mr Wilbram picked up his fork and started to

toy with the pudding. His normally pallid effigy of a face had already turned a rich, sweaty rose. At the same time it was restless, I thought, even melancholy.

By contrast Herr Untermeyer sucked at his lumps of pudding as eagerly as a baby sucks at a dummy-teat. Cream ran down his chin. Currants slipped from his spoon. His tongue, like that of an eager dog, leapt out and licked up morsels and dribbles with the deftness of a conjuror, with no pause for either word or breath.

Once Aunt Leonora remarked that it was a treat to see people eat. The pudding, I had to admit, was a poem, if rather a stolid one, and presently I began to feel my own face expanding, over-fed with rum, fruit, and cream, into a flushed, almost feverish bag, my eyes moist and somnolent.

With much scraping and sucking, Herr Untermeyer left his platter clean – licked would almost have been the appropriate word – and then, glass suddenly high, *schniffed* the *budding*, red lips spluttering a sentence half-English, half-German, in which I several times caught, I thought, the word 'engels'.

Aunt Leonora instantly demanded to know what all this meant and I, not really having more than the faintest idea myself, as instantly translated it as:

'Otto says the pudding could only have been made by the hands of angels.'

It might have been a trick I'd learned from her. It might have been one of her own inspired half-truths. At any rate with a cry of joy she jumped up from the table, waltzed round it to Otto and excitedly kissed him, continental fashion, on both cheeks. Then, before he had time to recover from this affectionate onslaught, she kissed him with what I thought was astonishingly vigorous ardour on the lips, saying:

'And that one's for the Zugspitze. For luck. For old times. Who says there's any lack of Anglo-German unity?'

My swift examination of Mr Wilbram's face found it far gone beyond melancholy. It was sunk in reproving gloom. At the same time his eye was arid. There were clearly excessive heights of passion towards which even Christmas pudding could not be permitted to reach. There were limits even to Anglo-German fellowship.

It wasn't surprising that, after all this, Otto took a second helping of pudding or that Aunt Leonora cut it even larger than the first. While he attacked it with that unremitting vigour Aunt Leonora found such a delight Uncle Freddie topped up the wine glasses, Otto at once seizing his and holding it aloft to *schniff* us all in general and the pudding again in particular, saying that he could only wish it was always Christmas in summer-time.

'In Germany we have never this. Never this festival in *sommer*.'

'Oh! who says anything about angels?' Aunt Leonora said. 'You're the angel if ever there was one. Oh! Otto, you haven't changed a bit. *Spoem*, remember?'

This new and sweeping word, this new marriage of German and English, suddenly fell on us, I thought, like an entrancing rocket.

'You remember *spoem*, surely, Otto?'

'*Bitte?*'

'It was the second night at the Hirschen. We'd all been drinking that wild raspberry drink. Not *framboise*, that's French. *Himber* or something like that, isn't it? We'd been drinking it for hours. Perhaps I was a little far gone, I don't know, but suddenly I turned to you and said 'S'lovely, isn't it? S'poem, isn't it?' *Spoem* – it became one of those words – *spoem*, like *schniff*, you know? *Spoem* – you surely remember?'

'*Bitte? Ah, so, so.*'

'Anyway,' she said, with one of those entrancing and wholly unexpected turns of mind that sometimes make her, in fact, a sort of *spoem* herself, 'who's for cheese?'

Uncle Freddie, Mr Wilbram and I were, reluctantly, not for cheese, but Otto was.

'Ah! the Stilton,' Aunt Leonora said. 'At the last moment I remembered it. There must be one more very, very English thing, I thought, and Stilton was it.'

While Aunt Leonora danced to the kitchen to fetch the Stilton

Uncle Freddie went to the sideboard and came back with a decanter.

'Well, if Stilton must be eaten,' he said, 'then port must be drunk. Agree, dear boy?'

I said I very much agreed and in the same moment saw Mr Wilbram take a quick, cold look at his watch. Then as Freddie started to find glasses for the port Mr Wilbram whispered something into Herr Untermeyer's ear and Herr Untermeyer looked at his watch too.

'*Ah ! so*. Fine, fine. Is plenty.'

'Ah! port!' Aunt Leonora came back into the room bearing dishes of butter and biscuits and a half Stilton. 'Splendid idea. Have we time?' She looked at her watch too. 'Oh! oceans, oceans. That little orchid trip won't take us the whisk of a donkey's tail.'

Here I thought it prudent to remind her that the orchids were not only rare but widely scattered, that their habitat was as jealously guarded as a state secret and that, in any case, the flowering season of many of them was already over; to which she replied, characteristically:

'Well, we don't expect to see all Rome in a day, do we? Of course we shan't see them all. That isn't the point. It's the feeling that they *might* be there.'

Herr Untermeyer attacked the Stilton. With an ardour undiminished he married it with the port. It was all, like the Kate and Sidney, the Christmas pudding and the *Deidesheimer Hofstück* '59, *schön*, the work of angels. Every moment he looked more richly, expansively content.

'A little more Stilton, Otto? Another drop of port? A *soupçon – kleine? –*'

Mr Wilbram, by this time, had grown visibly impatient. He didn't want to interrupt things, he said, coldly, but he felt he had to remind Mrs Elphinstone about the bus. The bus had to be christened. At five o'clock prompt. And afterwards representatives of the two towns had to take a ride in it and this too couldn't be delayed. Was this – this other – so important?'

'Of course, it's important.' She gave him one of those characteristically dark, accusatory glares of hers that had him silenced completely. 'It's important to show him our heritage and all that, isn't it? That's what he's here for, isn't he?'

It is always hard to reply to these caustic darts of Aunt Leonora's; they disarm the best of men; and Mr Wilbram remained miserably, but I thought wisely, silent.

'After all it is the little things that count. It's neglecting them that leads to wars.' After this astonishing statement of untruth she declared, rather sharply, that she would get the coffee. 'It's only a matter of a mile, anyway. Goodness gracious, it isn't a route march, is it? The walk will do us all the world of good.'

Our hills are not high; their grassy slopes, rich with cowslips in spring and light drifts of harebells in summer, have nothing in common with the slopes of the Zugspitze; but they rise with sudden abruptness, hard, dry bosoms of grass that present, to those who have just lunched well on two sorts of pudding, two of wine, Stilton cheese and coffee, obstacles as formidable as those in a steeplechase.

'We might possibly see the Spider,' Aunt Leonora said. We were all struggling up the steep rough hillside, she and Otto ahead together, I next, Mr Wilbram last, in single file, in the heat of afternoon. 'And the Bee. But not of course anything so rare as the Military. That's only known to a dozen or more choice spirits.'

I always admired certain phrases of Aunt Leonora's and 'choice spirits', I thought, was good.

'We are not seeing this military?' Herr Untermeyer stopped suddenly to say. 'This camp?'

'No, no, Otto. You don't quite understand. The Military is not a camp. It's a flower.'

'Not a camp? But this Romans? —'

'That,' she said, 'is quite a different matter.'

'So?'

'Left fork here !'

At the command Herr Untermeyer turned, stomping behind

Aunt Leonora up an even steeper path. Before I joined them something made me stop and look back. Twenty yards behind me, bent at the knees, head well down, Mr Wilbram had stopped for breath.

'Everything all right?' I called. 'Shall I wait for you?'

There was no sound in answer; Mr Wilbram merely waved one hand, flat, like a man counting a boxer out.

A minute or two later, as I climbed the path, I saw that Aunt Leonora and Herr Untermeyer had also paused. They seemed, I thought, to be having something of an argument. It became evident, presently, that Herr Untermeyer wasn't happy about the military. I heard him declare, rather aggressively, that he was confused, that he did not understood.

It was very hot and a slight breeze blowing from the sea only seemed to make the air more burning. But with a coolness I thought remarkable Aunt Leonora started to explain, clearly not for the first time, that the military on the one hand wasn't quite the same as the military on the other. To make it worse she explained that in any case we wouldn't see either.

'So? But Herr Wilbram is spoking of a camp.'

'I know Mr Wilbram spoke of a camp. But there is nothing to be seen. It has all disappeared. You can only stand on the spot and say "It was here". Or rather probably.'

'Ah! it is here?'

'No, no, it isn't here. It was probably a mile or two over there. There were probably two camps anyway.'

'Ah! two camps? This is why you are spoking of the military twice?'

In answer Aunt Leonora developed a sudden sharp concern for Mr Wilbram. Where was the man? She turned and looked back to where Mr Wilbram, practically on all fours now, seemed to be fumbling for the right fork in the path. Good God, she said, speaking as if the man were slacking, did he expect them to stand around and wait? They hadn't got all day.

Here I suggested that Mr Wilbram might perhaps be feeling the effects of lunch, particularly the puddings. Herr Untermeyer at once struck his chest a resounding blow.

'No, no, that can't be so. You are not feeling this *buddings*. Not here.' He struck his chest again. 'With the bestest cooking you are not feeling it. In one half hour it is not felt.'

With these praises falling enthusiastically on her ears Aunt Leonora positively purred.

'Shall we press on to the top then? Best foot forward. *Achtung*!'

Promptly Herr Untermeyer stomped ahead, now as it were in command, the *fuehrer* leading us. I felt warm sweat dribble down my hair into my neck and I turned to take yet another look at Mr Wilbram. His position on all fours seemed, I thought, to have become infinitely more acute, as if he had in fact resigned himself to the idea of crawling the rest of the way to the top.

'I think perhaps I ought to wait for Mr Wilbram,' I called.

'Oh! do no such thing. He'll catch up. He isn't tied to his mother's apron strings, is he? Press on!'

'Right,' I said. I started to press on. 'Excelsior!'

Herr Untermeyer, in spite of years, fat, puddings and port, pressed on too, climbing at a punishing pace. Even Aunt Leonora, inspired no doubt by memories of other, more youthful ascents, could hardly keep up. Nor in fact could I.

Far down the hillside Mr Wilbram crawled like a tortoise in pain. I paused once, looking back, to offer succour, but Mr Wilbram seemed merely to be sunk in an attitude of prayer.

By the time I reached the crest of the hillside Herr Untermeyer and Aunt Leonora were surveying the wide pastoral scene below them, its uttermost fringes pencilled with the faint line of the sea, with an air of triumphant satisfaction, almost if not quite smug.

'I said it was only a jaunt. I can't think why that man Wilbram makes so much fuss of it.'

'Herr Wilbram is tired? He does not seem to have the strong.'

Clearly Mr Wilbram had not the strong. A little concerned now, I made the suggestion that I should go back and help him to the top, an idea Aunt Leonora greeted with withering scorn.

'Good God, man, let him fend for himself. He'll be needing a rope next.'

Flabby-kneed, panting wretchedly, Mr Wilbram took nearly another five minutes to drag himself to the top, only to be greeted by Aunt Leonora, never the most tactful of women, saying:

'Well, you made it. Next time we'll bring an ice-axe.'

Herr Untermeyer laughed stentoriously. It was a laugh, fruity and slightly coarse, in which you could fairly hear the heavy power of puddings and it fell on Mr Wilbram, still periodically gasping for breath, like a mocking blow.

'I don't see that there's anything particularly funny about it.'

'No?' Herr Untermeyer merely let out another laugh, fruitier and coarser than the first.

'Oh! very well, if that's how you feel about it.'

Unexpectedly Herr Untermeyer now revealed a sense of humour hitherto entirely unexpected; or perhaps it was merely the good humour of the *Deidesheimer Hofstück* '59, the port and the flaming rum that was speaking.

'We should perhaps have brought a *dachshund*, eh, *mit* brandy?'

'I don't quite follow that remark,' Mr Wilbram said.

'*So?*' Herr Untermeyer laughed yet again, this time I thought a little loftily, with a touch of the master-race. 'On the great mountain you have the great *hund*. *St Bernard*. On the small mountain you have the small. You follow?'

Mr Wilbram did not follow; he turned, instead, very icy.

'Was that illustration meant as a personal affront,' he said, 'or what?'

'Oh! it was a bit of light-heartedness,' Aunt Leonora said.

'It was not exactly,' Mr Wilbram said, 'my idea of light-heartedness. But of course there's a difference between English and German humour.'

'Oh! is there? I never noticed it.'

'We are dragged up here on some – some pretext,' Mr Wilbram said, 'and I find myself laughed at. I say "we". All except Mr Elphinstone, of course. I noticed he didn't come.'

Hitherto no one had remarked on the absence of Uncle Freddie who, as was customary, had conveniently stayed behind to have a zizz.

'My husband has nothing to do with it. He always retires after lunch.'

'So do I.'

'Then,' she said with one of those wide, enchanting, large-toothed smile of hers, 'you should have said so.'

Mr Wilbram gasped impotently. Herr Untermeyer stood erect, very stiff. A train, crossing the valley far below, gave a sudden shrilling whistle, the sound ripping the warm still air.

'Men make such a song and dance about little things,' Aunt Leonora went on. 'You could have had a zizz too if you'd wanted to. You only had to say.'

'A what?'

'A zizz. A nap. Good gracious me, you might have thought we'd asked you to climb the Matterhorn.'

'Of course some of us,' Mr Wilbram said, 'have the advantage of being mountain climbers.'

'We were all so jolly and friendly,' she said, 'and then suddenly you went all spokey.'

'Spokey? I must saw you use the oddest words sometimes. What exactly does that mean?'

'It means,' I said, 'bloody-minded.'

'Oh! it does? Do you mind cutting out the bad language? I don't think that helps.'

I didn't say anything; I didn't think, at that moment, that anything would help. There was a feeling in the air, it seemed to me, of undeclared conflict. The forces of Anglo-German unity had drifted rather far apart.

'Well,' Aunt Leonora said, with remarkable poise and cordiality, 'shall we sort of drift back?'

I loved the expression 'sort of drift back'; but if it was intended as balm on the troubled air it failed completely.

'Oh! do exactly as you like,' Mr Wilbram said. 'Take no notice of me. I don't want to break up the afternoon.'

'Would you like to go back, Otto?' Aunt Leonora said. 'There'd be just time for a cup of tea.'

'I am thinking yet,' Herr Untermeyer said, 'of the military. This perhaps we have time to see?'

'No, no, Otto. I've already explained. There isn't any military. Except for the orchid. And that's quite different.'

'Exactly. Why don't you tell him,' Mr Wilbram said, 'that there aren't any orchids either? I don't want to press the point, but could we get back? We've got a bus to christen.'

Without waiting for an answer, Mr Wilbram started back down the hill. Aunt Leonora, under her breath, said she wished people wouldn't get so huffy and spokey and then, in a voice deliberately loud, said:

'Otto. Straight across there – right across – so far as you can see – is Hastings. Where the great battle was fought.'

'Oh! who cares about the Battle of Hastings?' Mr Wilbram said. 'We're late now.'

'I do for one,' she said. 'I care about it awfully. We wouldn't be the same without it, would we? It's part of our heritage, isn't it?' And then, in one of those delightfully diplomatic thrusts of hers: 'It might do a bit more good if you showed the flag.'

'Flag?' Mr Wilbram said. 'What flag?'

'Our flag. You were fast enough showing that German one.'

Oh! indeed and where was that? Mr Wilbram wanted to know.

'In that wretched paper. You were waving the German one and Otto had the Union Jack.'

'That,' Mr Wilbram said, 'is what it is all about. In case you've missed the point.'

'Oh! is it? Then I can only say it would have made more sense if you'd have waved ours instead of theirs. What next? I expect we'll all soon be waving the hammer-and-sickle.'

'Oh! my dear woman –'

For the second time Mr Wilbram started down the hillside. I thought it prudent to follow and then heard Otto say:

'This battle. This is the affair military we are coming to see?'

'No, no, Otto. We should go. You have your bus to christen.'

'You are speaking also of flags.'

'Well, yes, just in passing. Shall I lead the way?'

'Herr Wilbram is angry? Yes, I think. Why is Herr Wilbram angry?'

'I told him he was waving the wrong flag.'

'So? Which is the wrong flag?'

'The German flag.'

'So? You are not liking the German flag?'

There are moments when my Aunt Leonora, divine crackpot that she is, is capable of the most deliberate, endearing honesty.

'No,' she said. 'It does something to me. It curls me up inside.'

We descended the hillside in absolute silence. The heat of the sun, coming more from the westward now, seemed more burning than ever. A chalky dust rose from our footsteps. I now felt powerfully thirsty and, unlike Herr Untermeyer, could feel the two puddings engaged in heavy, sometimes windy, conflict inside me.

By the time we reached the foot of the hill some hidden force had conquered Mr Wilbram's lethargy. Armed with second wind, he was striding out strongly, fifty yards ahead. Long before we reached Aunt Leonora's house he had doubled the distance and by the time we reached it too he was already sitting, pale and impatient, at the wheel of his car.

'Wouldn't you all care for a cup of tea?'

'I'm afraid we haven't the time.'

'It won't take a minute. I'll have the kettle on in a jiff.'

'English tea?' Otto suddenly said. 'This I am liking very much. *Mit* toast, eh? This is something splendid.'

'Good. Then we'll all go in, shall we? Freddie'll be awake now.'

Perhaps the very thought of Freddie having been asleep all afternoon, deeply lapped in a zizz, roused some demon in Mr Wilbram. At any rate he suddenly thrust his head out of the window of his car and positively barked:

'Otto! *There is no time*!'

'You mean for tea?' Aunt Leonora spoke with the utmost sweetness, itself as maddening as anything could be, smiling blandly with those long teeth of hers. 'Of course there's time. There's oceans of time.'

'Otto, we must go. There simply isn't the time.'

'Oh! don't be such a fidget. Of course there's time.'

'I am not a fidget!'

'Then don't be so spokey. If Otto wants a cup of tea then he can have a cup of tea, can't he? Don't make such an issue of it.'

'I am not making an issue of it. But Herr Untermeyer has a programme to keep.'

'Then he must do a Francis Drake, mustn't he? Have a cup of tea with plenty of time to beat the Spaniards afterwards –'

'Otto! We haven't the time. *We must get going*. Spaniards! –'

Otto was already half-way up the garden path, with Aunt Leonora not far behind. As if this were not irritation enough in itself the front door of the house suddenly opened and Uncle Freddie appeared, fresh and vibrant from sleep, eager with smiling welcome.

'Ah! there you all are. Tongues hanging out, I expect. I've got the kettle on.'

I suppose it was 'tongues hanging out' that provided the last extreme force that unloosed the puritanical demon in Mr Wilbram. Suddenly he yapped like an infuriated dog:

'Once and for all, Otto, we have to go.' He was actually out of the car now. Paler than ever, he strode as far as the garden gate. 'For heaven's sake, don't you realize it's nearly five o'clock? Why on earth must you have tea?'

'Because I am thirsty.'

'Then get Mrs Elphinstone to give you a glass of water and let's get going. Quickly.'

'Glass of water, my foot,' Aunt Leonora said. 'The man's entitled to tea if he wants to have tea, isn't he? Without being bossed around.'

'The tea I am taking only in small portion. Most quickly. In one moment.'

Mr Wilbram banged with his fists on top of the garden gate, shouting:

'Otto, if you don't come now, I wash my hands of the whole affair. I disclaim responsibility. We shall only be just in time as it is. It's on your head, I warn you, it's on your head.'

Herr Untermeyer too strode to the garden gate.

'You are spoking very loud at me?'

'I am and I will!'

'Ah! *so?* You wish conflict?'

'I am not talking of conflict. I am talking of time. Getting to places on time. People are waiting. Don't you understand?'

'I do not understand when you are making loud words!'

'Now, now,' Aunt Leonora said. 'You two. You mustn't get at loggerheads.'

'Loggerheads?' Otto said. 'Loggerheads? What is this word? Explain to me, please.'

'Oh! damn the explaining! I don't often use strong language, but really, really! Damn the word! Damn the man! –'

'This word I am knowing. This damn. This is not polite.'

'Oh! it's an everyday word nowadays,' Aunt Leonora said. 'Nobody takes any notice. Like bloody. Anyway, you shouldn't swear at your visitor, Mr Wilbram, should you?'

'I am not swearing at him!' Mr Wilbram actually shook his fist in the air. 'I am simply saying that if he doesn't come now, this minute, I'll wash my hands of the whole affair.'

'Oh! why don't you all come in?' Uncle Freddie called from the doorway. 'The tea's already made.'

'I come!' Otto said. 'The tea I will take at once! Like *blitzen* – quick take!'

'You will do no such thing. We've had to deal with this German obstinacy before,' Mr Wilbram explained. 'This wretched Teutonic – whatever it is –'

'Bloody-mindedness,' I said.

'Well, whatever it is! The only way is to treat with obstinacy in return. I say we go now! I say no tea! You understand?'

'I understood. You wish conflict again, ah? This is catastroff!'

Herr Untermeyer actually raised his fist and shook it so aggressively that I thought he would, for one moment, poke Mr Wilbram in the eye. The two men faced each other, one red with passion, one pale with ashen indignation, both speechless, at a point of thunderflash, until suddenly my Aunt Leonora said with disarming sweetness:

'Into the car, the pair of you. The tea-party can wait until some other time. We don't want another Boston on top of us, do we?'

Like two scowling dogs, anger unappeased, Mr Wilbram and Herr Untermeyer got into the car.

'Good-bye, Otto,' Aunt Leonora said, almost as if nothing had happened. '*Auf Wiedersehen.* You won't be late. It's been like old times. Come again.'

'It is catastroff!' I heard Herr Untermeyer say. 'Catastroff!'

The car drove away. The pair of hands that waved the briefest of farewells, one German, one English, were scarcely flags of cordiality.

Slowly I walked back to the house with Aunt Leonora. Above us the hills were bathed in serenity. The golden summer air was utterly silent. Nothing could have been more peaceful. Only she herself seemed, for once, I thought, more than a little perturbed.

'I wouldn't have expected that from Otto,' she said at last and her voice was hurt. 'Why did he have to behave like that? It wasn't like him at all. It wasn't a bit like he used to be. I do wish people wouldn't change so. It would make it so much easier if they always remained the same, don't you think?'

As I looked back at the tranquil hills, in the golden August sun, it was suddenly on the tip of my tongue to say that the chords of youth were very tender; but I kept quiet instead, content to know that I had no answer.

The White Wind

THE lagoon had the hot brilliance of a stretch of celluloid constantly ignited by sunlight into white running flame. From far beyond it the Pacific galloped ceaselessly, charging, white-maned, against the coral reef. At each point of the gap, where the swell poured in, flew great conical flags of splendid spume.

'Does the boat go fast?'

'Like the wind.'

'How fast?'

'Like the wind, boy. I told you. Like the wind.'

In the shadowy shed, half tin, half palm-frond, the boy fed into a strange rattling wheel-like contraption, not unlike a roundabout at a fair, another soda-water bottle. The machine filled it, sealed it with a sound like that of gnashing iron teeth and bore it away.

'How long to go to Papeete in the boat?'

'No time.'

'And Bora-Bora?'

'No time. Just like the wind, I tell you. No time.'

On the far side of the machine sat a mass of yellow indolence on a box. It stretched out at mechanical intervals a soporific crab-like hand that grasped the filled soda-water bottles and dropped them in a crate. It had grown over the years so completely into the lethargy of this rhythm that occasionally, when it fell asleep in the heat of oppressive afternoons, the hand kept up its fat, slow clawing, independently.

The boy knew this mass of odiously distended flesh as Fat Uncle. He knew of no other name than Fat Uncle.

'Fat Uncle, is the boat faster than Pierre's?'

'Pierre, Pierre, who's Pierre? Boat? – you call that a boat? That fish barrel?'

The flesh of the face was so solidly inflated, like a hard tyre, that the simple eyes appeared in it merely as two long slits nicked there by a knife held in a hand that had grown suddenly unsteady as it traced the left-hand eye.

This eye seemed not only larger than the other. It slanted upwards and backwards, jaggedly. The appearance achieved by it was one of idiotic cunning. It was then repeated, astonishingly, in the centre of the naked, soapy paunch below. There the navel lay like a third snoozing eye, the creased lid of stomach folding across it, heaving deeply up and down.

The boy's own eyes were black and listening. He was slightly over four feet in height, rather squat, with thick yellow skin and a mat of black shining hair that was never combed. There was nothing in these rather inconspicuous features to distinguish him from a score of other boys who ran about the water-front except the eyes. They were far-seeing, arrested, solemn eyes and they were inclined to fix themselves for long periods on distances away at sea, without the trace of a smile.

When he was not working with Fat Uncle at the soda-water machine he spent most of his time working and running errands about the port for an American named Edison. Edison owned, among other things, the soda-water plant. He also owned the tin-hut, Fat Uncle, the schooner that Fat Uncle said was as fast as the wind and a hotel on the water-front.

'Faster than the wind,' Fat Uncle sometimes said. 'Faster. Like a hurricane.'

The hotel was a broken-down weather-boarded building with a balustraded upper verandah and a number of open cubicles for drinkers facing the street below. The outside had not been painted for many years but the cubicles inside were raw with violent scarlet, freshly painted, impressed here and there with what seemed like crude transfers of Polynesian girls, with purple *leis* about their necks and green and yellow bark-shirts, dancing.

Edison was fond of purple. Most days he wore a purple shirt, sometimes with large designs of dragons across it, sometimes with rosettes of vast, purple flowers. This colour threw into sickly relief the thin, balding head, the long neck and the scooped dark cheeks with their two-day beard.

On Saturday nights, when the boy spent most of his time
helping a Chinaman to wash glasses in the kitchen at the back
of the hotel, Edison thumped away at an out-of-tune piano, Fat
Uncle played a ukelele and the floor between the cubicles thun-
dered with sweating, stampeding dancers. In the wild heat of
these Saturdays the boy heard men mouthing across the floor
untranslatable violent slogans, sometimes in English, sometimes
in French, which he did not understand, and occasionally in his
own language, which he merely thought he did. Somehow he
knew that these were dirty men.

At night he dropped to sleep in the shed. He did not mind
the shed. He was in fact very glad of the shed. The shed had
become an almost solitary means of comfort to him. It reminded
him always of Fat Uncle and the boat, the schooner that went
faster than the wind. Sometimes too there was a bottle of soda
water that had not been properly sealed and at night he lay
down in the warm darkness and drank it, chewing a little raw
fish at the same time, or a little coconut.

Occasionally Edison got hold of a sucking pig, invited people
to the hotel and gave a big meal, with dishes of hot rice, fish
salad, tuna, bread-fruit, shrimps and yams. After it was over
the boy could sometimes find among the dishes a few unchewed
ribs of pork that he could take away to the shed and gnaw there
like a dog.

Over and over again, during the day time, he found some
chance to speak with Fat Uncle about the schooner.

'How long was the schooner yours?'

'Years. Years.'

'Why did you sell her to Edison?'

'Bad luck, boy. Bad luck. We all have bad luck sometimes.'

The accumulated effect of these conversations on the boy was
one of wonder. Even when a sudden elephantine hand struck
out at him because the soda-water machine had jammed he
was aware of no resentment, no bitterness, against Fat Uncle.

For some reason these blows seemed always to strike him on
the right-hand side of the face, so that his head appeared to have
developed a slight and permanent list to one side. It was this list

that gave to his eyes the remarkable impression that he was always listening to half-formed, distant sounds. It deepened his air of being fascinated. It made him seem to regard Fat Uncle as a sort of demi-god, part sinister but full of gripping, fathomless sources of wonder.

'Did you once take her to the Marquesas?'

'Once? Once? About a million times!'

'Samoa? You said you once took her to Samoa.'

'Samoa — I took her everywhere. Over the whole Pacific. The whole world, I tell you. The whole world. Everywhere.'

'Tell me about Samoa.'

In Samoa, Fat Uncle said, the men were big and vain. The villages were neat and pretty, with big round huts of palm. There was much cocoa, a lot of copra. Lazy and easy, the voyages to Samoa, to pick up cocoa. Good profits. Plenty of dough.

'Where is Noumea? You said you once took her to Noumea.'

The yellow crab-like fingers would wave with exhausted disdain in a direction vaguely westerly.

'A million miles that way.'

As he spoke of these distances, totally incomprehensible to the boy, who had never even sailed beyond the reef, he would actually open his eyes to their full simple width, as if the very fact of their being open was proof of candour, and then wave his hand again.

'Look at her. You'd thing a man would take her out sometimes, wouldn't you? A man who was a man.'

A great hand would grab with bloated impatience at a soda-water bottle. A great mouth, with scornful looseness, would spit at the floor.

'Look at her. By God, only look at her.'

On the dingy water-front, from which every turn of wind licked up from the many pot-holes a darting tongue of dust, the schooner lay squat and desolate, listing to one side. She had all the beauty of a floating hen-house dragged from the sea.

'Goes like the wind, I tell you. Like a bird.'

As he stared at the schooner and listened to these things the boy ceased to exist as a mere half-naked figure in the shed. He walked out into a great world of water and islands beyond the reef, beyond the farthest rim of horizon, and found that Fat Uncle was king of it.

The discovery, for all its wonder, was incomplete in itself. He knew it could never be complete until he himself was part of it. And always, at night, in the shed, he would lie for some time awake, however tired he was, openly dreaming, trying to think of devious situations in which Edison, by some miracle, would one day take the schooner out of the harbour and beyond the towering reef, to distant places.

'Couldn't you buy the boat back from Edison?'

'Me? What with? It's his. He owns it. He should take it out.'

'It's a pity you sold it.'

'A pity – too true it was. Everything was going well. And then there it was. Suddenly. Like I told you. Bad luck. I wanted the money. Every man has bad luck sometimes.'

'Perhaps one day Edison will have bad luck.'

'You tell me why. Edison's always had the luck. You tell me why.'

There were times, in more fabulous moments of memory, when Fat Uncle also spoke of fish.

'Until you get out there –' the disdaining obese fingers waved to the far corners of the world – 'you've never seen a fish. They're like ships, the fish there. Like ships. The sharks have mouths like doors.'

'And the wind? You said once about the wind.'

'The wind will drive you for days. Weeks sometimes. Down to Australia before you can catch a rope or get your breath or turn a hair.'

'Do you wish you were out there again? With the big fish? With the big wind?'

'Wish it? By God, wish it ! –'

It ended one morning with Fat Uncle kicking over the crate of soda-water bottles, grabbing up a bottle as he passed and then heaving himself in outrage, blowing hoarsely, towards the door, to emerge there like an obese blanched maggot hunching itself from the dark core of a rotting fruit, half-blinded by sunshine.

'I gave her away. That's the truth of it. I should have got three times as much for her. Four times as much. I gave her away. Six times. He got her out of me.'

He sucked coarsely at the soda-water bottle like a vast baby tugging at a glassy teat.

'I could prove he got her out of me. Six times as much – that's what I should have got for her.'

'You said once the wind blew you for ten days. Were you frightened?'

'Of a thing like that?' He laughed his cackling, simple-minded laugh. 'The sea's your friend. I was never frightened. It never does to be frightened.'

In the complication of feeling that the schooner was beautiful, that Fat Uncle was never frightened and that Edison was a person of sinister design who had achieved the unforgivable outrage of robbing Fat Uncle of the schooner and laying her up to rot, the boy stood staring at the lagoon with solemn musing eyes.

A girl in a white and crimson *pereu*, hatless, with a single yellow hibiscus darting a pistil tongue from her waist-length blue-black hair, walked a moment later across the water-front, away from the hotel.

'Ginette, Ginette.' The fat lips of Fat Uncle sucked the name in and out, grossly, as they had sucked at the soda-water bottle. 'Look at her. Ginette. They all love to call themselves by French names. Where do you suppose she's hurrying off to?'

'To get fish.'

'Fish. Fish.' The squelching lips made noises of scorn. 'Perhaps he's a man with her, eh? Perhaps even half a man –'

The boy, without warning, suddenly lifted his face. The eyes, darting sideways, caught out of the glittering sky, from the south, a half-formed distant sound.

A moment later he was running. His voice leapt out in a sudden little yell of surprise that made the girl in the *pereu*, walking across the dusty pot-holes of the water-front, suddenly halt and turn, as if he had yelled for her to wait for him.

'It's the day for the little plane,' he was shouting. 'The day for the little plane.'

The girl had disappeared by the time he reached the end of the water-front, where a belt of palms, very tall, sprang out of a shore of graphite-coloured sand. Beyond these palms the airstrip opened out, a dusty stretch of uneven grass across which the plane was taxi-ing, wings dipping up and down, like a bird faking a wound and limping for cover.

The boy looked more than ever inconspicuous under the tall thin palms, the fronds of which began to flap above him like steel feathers as the little plane, taxi-ing in, stirred up currents of air with its dusty slip-stream.

From the plane came two men, the older, taller one spectacled and rubbery, in crumpled grey suit, carrying a brown leather bag, the smaller with a pigskin brief-case under his arm, neat and studious, with immaculate white shirt and shorts and thin white stockings.

The boy ran towards these men with excitement, waving both hands in greeting.

'Dr Gregory! Monsieu' Longuemart! Dr Gregory!'

Dr Gregory, the rubbery, spectacled American, waved a hand in reply. The Frenchman merely smiled at the sight of the boy stumbling down towards the air-strip and it was Gregory who called:

'Hi, Timi! How are you? What goes?'

He held out a cool greyish hand to grip the boy's dusty palm and the boy in turn held out his other hand to grasp the bag.

'I may carry the bag?'

'One of these days the bag will carry you.'

'Please?'

'Never mind. Skip it,' the doctor said. 'Have you been a good boy? That's the thing. Did you take your pills?'

'Yes, doctor.'

'All of them? How many left?'

'Four. I'd forgotten it was today you came.'

'Good boy.'

The boy walked the rest of the way to the water-front be-tween the Frenchman and the American. The Frenchman was speechless, reserved and smiling. It was always the American who talked.

'Did Ginette take her pills?'

'I think so.'

'Anybody else you know take them? What about Fat Uncle?'

'He was going to take them one night and then he went fishing. Another day he was sick.'

'Where? How sick?'

'Here.'

The boy put his hand on his stomach. The doctor said, 'They are always sick, aren't they?' and the Frenchman, to whom the remark was really addressed, smiled, a little more broadly this time.

'Have you been sick?'

'No, doctor.'

They were by now on the water-front, in sight of the short cluster of houses, the schooner and the hotel.

'I see Pierre's boat isn't here,' the doctor said. 'Where's Pierre?'

'I think he has taken the boat to Apia,' the boy said. 'He went yesterday.'

As they walked the rest of the distance down the water-front the doctor felt a sudden compulsion to muse aloud to the Frenchman.

'One of these days they'll be in a fine jam here. Pierre will have the boat in Apia or Suva or somewhere and we won't have the biplane fixed and something'll break out and there'll be a fine mess. Like the epidemic on Bora-Bora. There'll be hell to pay.'

He waved seemingly tired loose-jointed hands at house-fences on which trailed creepers of tender golden bells. His grey, rather globular eyes rested on bright barriers of red ginger-lily and hibiscus, the hibiscus full blown, crimson and yellow, but still unshrivelled by glaring sun.

'Beautiful, isn't it?' the doctor said. 'Incredibly beautiful. I must get some pictures before I go back. I've got a batch of new slides. Look at the crotons. They always remind me of snakes, those yellow ones. They come out well in colour.'

They presently drew level with Edison's schooner, the semi-derelict hen-house rocking gently up and down against the wooden water-front piles, and the doctor stopped to regard her with a certain ironic sadness.

'All so beautiful, Jean, but no telephone.'

Gazing from the schooner, he turned with shrugged shoulders to the Frenchman.

'How do you like your lines of communication?'

The Frenchman, staring at the schooner, smiled too and also ironically.

'She goes like the wind,' the boy said.

'Does she now? Who says so?'

'Fat Uncle. Faster than the wind. She goes faster than the wind.'

'Does she?' the doctor said.

He strode out, too affected to look at the boy, feeling it time to move on. He rested a hand on the boy's shoulder, as if in comfort or tenderness, or merely confidentially. 'So you haven't been sick? Nothing? Not once?'

'No, doctor.'

'And you know why you haven't been sick?'

'Yes, doctor.'

'Why?'

'Because I take the pills.'

'Good boy,' the doctor said.

They were already within fifty yards of the hotel. Abruptly the doctor stopped again, eyes protuberant with moderately pained disgust as he stared at Edison's crumbling frontage.

'How do you suppose it holds up?' he said. 'The only good thing about it is the soda-water. Every time I come here I expect to see it flat. Which way do you suppose it would fall, Jean? On its face or on its backside?'

The Frenchman spoke with meticulous, pointed effect for the first time.

'On its knees, I hope.'

'Yes? I suppose a short prayer would do it no harm,' the doctor said.

The first of these ironic flippancies was lost on the boy. He understood the doctor only when he spoke of pills. In a simple illustration, months before, the doctor had made him understand, perfectly and for all time, the meaning of the pills.

'I want you to look at this. The picture of a girl. Do you think she's beautiful?' The doctor, who was fond of photography, had drawn from his case a coloured slide. The boy held the translucent glass to the light and gazed at it. 'Yes, she is beautiful. Something like Ginette,' he said. The doctor retrieved the slide and held out another. 'Now look at this. Would you think, perhaps, she was the same girl?'

'No. Not the same girl.'

'Why not?'

'She looks very old and she has the elephant legs.'

'She is the same girl,' the doctor said. 'She has the elephant legs. Only ten months later.'

After this the doctor took him by the hands. The doctor's loose large-jointed fingers were surprisingly cool and tender.

'Nothing like that can happen to you if you take the pills,' he said. 'You understand? Nothing can ever happen to you.'

They were by now outside the front of the hotel. The doctor and the Frenchman went inside and sat at one of the scarlet cubicles, followed by the boy. 'I guess a gin-fizz is called for,' the doctor said. 'Perhaps two gin-fizzes.' White globes of sweat from the short exertion of the walk had begun to drip from his face and neck and chest and with a large white handkerchief he started to mop them away.

'Tell Edison two gin-fizzes,' he said to the boy. 'Two really nice long gin-fizzes. Special ones.'

'Special ones,' the boy said. 'Yes, doctor,' and moved away from the cubicle.

It was the girl and not Edison who eventually brought the gin-fizzes, carrying them in on a round bamboo tray.

'Ginette,' the doctor said and both he and the Frenchman half-rose from their seats in greeting.

'Eddo will be here in a minute. Oh! don't get up.' Her mouth, red and rather full, broke at once and for no reason at all into bright beating laughter. 'He's in a temper at me because I was late getting the fish.'

'Please sit down,' the doctor said. 'Have a drink with us.'

'Oh! no, I'm quite happy.'

She laughed again, too readily and too loudly, the doctor thought, with head thrown back, thick red tongue quivering in the broad but pretty mouth.

'The boy could get it.'

'Oh! no, I'm really quite happy.'

She sat down. The doctor could not help admiring, as he always did, the sumptuous golden arms, the primitively sensational shoulders rising smooth and naked from the cavern of blue-black hair, as she leaned her elbows on the table and laughed splendidly again, for the third time. There was always something extraordinarily lovable, simple and touching, he thought, about that laughter. But today it struck him as being not only physically rich and splendid but also, in some way he hadn't yet fathomed, uneasily sad.

'Well, have a drink of mine,' he said.

She laughed again.

'Well, all right, doctor, a drink of yours.' She picked up the long glass and half looked at the doctor, then the Frenchman, through the rim of it. '*Santé!*' She drank gin-fizz, very briefly. 'How long do you stay?'

'It depends,' the doctor said, 'on how good people are. If they take their pills. Did you take your pills?'

'Of course.'

'If they were all as good as you,' the doctor said, 'we'd be away the same afternoon.'

'Then I'm glad they're not all as good as me.'

This was the signal for new and louder laughter and this time the doctor and the Frenchman joined in.

The laughter had hardly died away before Edison appeared in

sloppy purple shirt, sky-blue trousers and a growth of beard that was like a pale sandy scrubbing brush.

Slouching, he shook hands loosely with the doctor and the Frenchman, and then sat down, scratching his bare chest.

'Fish salad all right?' he said. 'Raw fish? All I can do today. I know you always like it.'

'Fine,' the doctor said.

'Might get a sucking pig next time you come,' Edison said, 'and Ginette'll get some shrimps. She'll do that favourite curry of yours.'

Suddenly Edison got up, went to the corner bar, beyond the cubicle, and poured himself a neat deep whisky to which he added a gill of soda. Then he came back to the cubicle, bringing the bottle and drinking from the glass as he walked along. It was a favourite habit of his.

'Fit?' the doctor said. 'I'll bet you didn't take those pills?'

'No,' Edison said, 'and you know I never will. Whites don't get elephantiasis. You know that.' He held up his glass. 'This is my bug-killer. Served me well and faithfully, man and boy, for many years.'

The doctor looked away. He was not anxious to pursue any further the discussion of a subject on which he was aware he was liable to grow distastefully fanatical when roused. He stared instead at Edison's schooner, moored across the waterfront.

'I see Pierre's away. What do you do for supplies when Pierre's not here?'

'Oh! people call. Boats. You'd be surprised.'

'Something you'd like when we come next time?'

'Don't think so,' Edison said. 'We always manage. Nothing ever happens here.'

'Supplies of bug-killer good?'

'Splendid. Never been exhausted yet.'

It pained the doctor to sit through the remainder of the drinks, through lunch and through some minutes of coffee afterwards, during which Edison lowered the level of the whisky bottle by several further inches and Ginette laughed at every other sentence or so. He did not know why he now felt un-usually discomforted and pained at the impression of some rift between the drinking Edison and the laughing girl, but his heart felt curiously sore and sick whenever he looked at her.

He found relief in praising the coffee. The only really tolerable thing about Edison, he thought, was the coffee.

It was really quite remarkable coffee that Edison made. Per-haps, in relief, he praised it over-generously:

'This is not only the best coffee in the islands. It's the best coffee in the world.'

'I know it.'

'It's nectar. It's perfect. You could never ask for anything better.'

'And you tell *me* how to live,' Edison said. 'On pills.'

Only a sense of irony kept anger pinned at the back of the doctor's throat.

'I don't tell you how to live,' he said. 'I don't tell you how to die either.'

He was relieved and glad to escape to the soda-water bottling shed, where he found the boy feeding bottles into the rattling roundabout and the indolent yellow mass of Fat Uncle respond-ing mechanically, three-parts asleep, in the oppressive afternoon.

He shook hands with the massive bloated mountain and, while Longuemart got ready a notebook in which to record figures, if there were any figures to record, introduced the sub-ject of pills.

Pain and nausea, with actual imitations of the process of vomiting, sprang sweatily from Fat Uncle's face. The slits of eyes actually opened, dark with simple despair.

'Sick,' Longuemart said. 'He's been very sick, he says. For several days.'

Gregory did not bother to use his own bad French, but said simply, in English:

'Give him two pills. Explain to him that the boy takes the pills.'

Longuemart, in French, explained this, at the same time holding out the pills. The eyes of Fat Uncle rolled open and then shut themselves tightly. The big soapy hands groped at the air like shaggy spiders crawling up and down invisible webs.

'He says he's sick enough already. The pills made him vomit twice as much. He cannot eat his food.'

'Hurt his pride,' the American doctor said. 'Shame him. Ask him if he wants to be thought less courageous than the boy.'

Fat Uncle held out his hands, flatly this time, in an appealing gesture of mute despair and Longuemart took the opportunity of placing the pills in the right-hand palm. Fat Uncle recoiled as if cut, speaking quickly.

'He says it is not a question of being as courageous as the boy. He knows the boy is very courageous but he is also younger. He says youth is everything. It never knows what it is to be tormented.'

'Tell him – no, don't bother.'

In despair, too, mildly tormented himself, the American suddenly gave up.

'We'll talk to him tomorrow before we leave,' he said. 'Give the boy his quota.'

The boy, with one of his rare smiles, held up his hands for the pills. Gregory patted him on the shoulder, smiling and saying:

'See you later, Timi. Ask Ginette to find me a water-melon.'

Together the two doctors started walking up the slight incline at the back of the hotel, away from the water-front. A sun like a burnished wheel flared down nakedly on that part of the road where there was no shade of palms. Its force struck the American with such unexpected brutality after the shade of the hut that he paused suddenly on the hillside to pass his hand across his face. He was a great believer in the virtues of tabulation. He was a firm worshipper of efficiency. As a consequence he had made up his mind to record every house on the island, to give it a number and to make up a case-history of every inhabitant, giving them numbers too. It would take many weeks, but he was determined to see it through.

'Where do we start today?' he said.

'House number four. Just along the road. Three Chinese. Numbers thirty-seven, thirty-eight and thirty-nine – S.'

The S, the doctor was aware, stood for Suspect. He twisted loose fingers across his chin. He was suddenly oppressed by heat, by the meaningless mass of trivial details which he himself had helped to devise and which now seemed of less consequence than the occasional snaking curls of dust that a light hot sea-wind blew from the pot-holes.

He looked back down the hill, towards the scrubby waterfront, the hotel, and the flat dust road running beside the lagoon. He could just make out the shape of the little plane on the edge of the air-strip and it was as if, for a moment, he wanted or had decided to go back to it.

'Something the matter? Did you mean to bring your camera?'

The American shook his head, seeming to sniff something. Cursorily he gave another glance at the hotel, so insubstantial-looking and tinder-like that he would not have been surprised to see it at any moment suddenly crumble or ignite in the torrid air.

'I just thought I smelled corruption,' he said. 'That's all.'

With increasing despair Gregory followed the Frenchman along the dust track by the lagoon at noon the following day. Both men were riding bicycles, the only form of transport, apart from horses, the island knew. The further bay of the island was too far away for walking and the American already felt exhausted as he tried to plough the bicycle along a track that the past rainy season had left like a scoured river-bed.

All morning his mind had been alight with irritating warning signals about the perils of inefficiency. His entire training and nationality revolted against the mere notion of mess. He disliked the idea of riding a bicycle not so much for its own power to discomfort but because his mind clamoured constantly that there must be some simpler, more efficient, less sweatily wasteful way of achieving the same end.

He got off the bicycle.

'Jean.' The Frenchman, riding ahead, turned and got off his

bicycle too. 'Jean – do you think you could manage here by yourself for a time?'

'I think so.'

'Perhaps a week? Maybe ten days?'

'I think so. Why?'

The American raised loose irritated hands and let them fall deprecatingly back on the handlebars of the bicycle.

'Two successes, ten failures, four pill-spitters and one who actually palmed it,' he said. 'We're great. We move mountains.'

'The vale of prejudice.'

'We've got to re-attack,' the American said. 'Re-form, I mean to say. If we're even going to reduce the incidence of this thing, let alone stamp it out, we'll only begin to do it by efficiency. And riding bicycles isn't efficiency.'

'Nor is it a cure for filariasis.'

The doctor, though fond of the Frenchman's habit of talking sense with light flippancy, did not smile.

'I'm going to take the plane back,' he said, 'and get scooter engines fitted to the bicycles.'

'You think they will prove more effective than pills?'

'I've got another idea in my mind, too,' he said, 'but first the bicycles.'

He actually turned his bicycle round in the track and stood with one foot on the pedal, preparing to get on.

'It'll take a few days to work out,' he said. 'But if you wouldn't mind staying on here –'

'Of course. Not at all.'

'Let's get back then. We'll have lunch and then load the bicycles into the *Rapide* and I'll be away.'

Riding back to the hotel the American, less oppressed by the guilt and irritations of inefficiency now that he had expressed his thoughts about it, found himself sometimes glancing from side to side. Beyond the masses of bright yellow and carmine crotons, with their twisted elegance that he was so fond of photographing, and beyond the rampant hedges of hibiscus and ginger-lily and creeper and the trees of *tiare* and jasmine that would smell more and more exquisitely as dusk came on, lay the stilted huts of palm-thatch that he knew so well. Above the huts spread the palms; and below the palms ran the little streams, open sewers, crossed here and there by crumbling bridges, that did not smell so exquisitely in the heat of noon. Under the palms, with their fallen coconuts, ran the rats, eating at the coconuts. Into the half-eaten nuts fell the rain and in the cups of rain bred the mosquitoes. That was his constant, evil cycle. With a revulsion that never lessened with each experience of it he longed to sweep it all away.

From one of the huts a half-Chinese woman, seeing the two doctors bicycling past, rattled with a length of bamboo on the edge of a tin roof, attracting their attention, calling something at the same time.

'What does she say?' the American said.

The Frenchman alighted from the bicycle and stood listening.

'Something about someone being ill there.'

'Did we call there already?'

'We called there yesterday. But there was no answer. We thought they were out. Fishing.'

It did not seem to the American worth the bother of getting off the bicycle. The pattern was one, he thought, he knew too well.

'Getting sick in readiness for us,' he said. 'Sickness is better than cure. We know that one.'

'Ought I perhaps to go in?'

The woman again shouted something as the American bicycled on.

'Come back after lunch. It's only five minutes,' he said. 'Tell her you'll be back in an hour. Tell her to stay there.'

At lunch the American was pleased to see the melon, a sugary-golden variety, with black frosty seeds, that the boy had told Ginette to get for him. Edison's coffee was again quite beyond praise and the only trace of the doctor's irritations of the morning arose from the fact that the coffee was too hot to drink as quickly as he wanted.

'I'll be back in a few days,' he said to Edison. 'At the most a week. Was there something you wanted?'

'Hell, no,' Edison said. 'I keep telling you. We've got everything here.'

'Including yaws, T.B., three sorts of –' the doctor started thinking and then checked himself abruptly. There was no time, even for the sake of candour, he told himself, to get himself involved in newer, further irritations. He would even decline, he thought, to take too much notice of how drunk Edison was, much drunker than at noon the previous day; or that on the face of the girl the sense of rift that had troubled him so sorely at yesterday's lunch had grown more pressing and more mystifying, a sharper pain.

'Do you wish me to ride the other bicycle to the plane with you?' Longuemart said, 'or could someone else perhaps ride it? I ought to get back to that woman. I think I ought to see what's the trouble there.'

'Timi can ride the bicycle,' the American said. 'The boy can ride it. If that's O.K. with Eddo?'

'Everything's O.K.,' Edison said.

'I'll come down to the plane with you,' the girl said suddenly, 'I'd like to. I'll ride the bicycle.'

Riding the bicycle along the water-front to the air-strip beyond the belt of palms the doctor noticed that the girl hardly spoke at all. He could not help admiring, once again, as he always did, her sumptuous strength as she helped him load the bicycle into the little plane; but he was inexplicably touched too by the brooding rift in her face, by the emotion in the broad, quivering nose, and he said, just before preparing to climb into the cockpit:

'Like to come to Papeete? Room for you if you cared to come.'

'No, thank you.'

'Would do you good. Nice for you.'

'No, thank you.'

Before speaking again the doctor performed once again his sudden trick of sniffing at air. He looked instinctively along the water-front in the direction of the crumbling hotel and thought that, once more, as yesterday, he caught a sudden smell of corruption in the air.

'Is something the matter?' he said.

From the cavernous mass of her dark hair, turning her face away, she looked down at the dust of the air-strip, not answering.

'Is something wrong?' he said. He was moved to put his hand on her shoulder.

'I know something's wrong because you laughed too much yesterday.'

'He is taking another vahini,' she said. 'That's all.'

Half an hour later she was still standing on the air-strip, gazing across the empty sky above the lagoon, as if half-hoping that the *Rapide* would for some reason appear and come back, when Dr Longuemart suddenly came running along the water-front at an agitated trot.

'Has it gone? Has Gregory gone?'

The stupidity of the question, aimed at an air-strip quite empty except for herself, made him stop short, white as his own shirt with exhaustion, panting self-reproaches.

'I might have caught him if I'd had another bicycle,' he said. 'But I couldn't find Eddo. I might have caught him —'

She stared at him with sudden bitterness.

'I could have told you where Eddo is,' she said. 'Why do you want the doctor? What's wrong?'

With difficulty the young Frenchman pulled his words together.

'There are three cases of typhoid in that house,' he said. 'And two in another.'

On the floor of the shed, in the stifling heat of the afternoon, Fat Uncle slept like a tired ape. The machine had stopped. The boy was dozing too.

Half dreaming, he could hear nothing but the sound of the Pacific beating against the reef. Of all the sounds in his life it was the one he heard least consciously. It simply beat through the days without rest, so that he heard it only as he might have heard the constant and ceaseless tick of a clock on a wall.

It occurred to him suddenly in this half-dream that the sea had begun to speak to him with several voices. Across the hot air these voices were arguing with complexity about something, uplifted.

He listened for several minutes, slowly waking, and then got up. It was not until he reached the door of the hut that he realized that the sea, or the envelope of hot dead air enclosing the sea, had played on him the oddest of tricks. The voices were real voices. He could in fact already hear Edison's voice among them, louder than the rest, and they came from inside the hotel.

He walked across the yard. Between the yard and the cubicles that faced on to the water-front was a kitchen where cockroaches as large as mice ran for cover when the evening lamp was lit and where a lean and almost hairless Chinaman prepared fish and vegetables, cooked and washed up dishes. This Chinaman too was asleep, his head resting on the comparatively cool edge of the sink, one yellow hand on a tap, as if in the act of turning it.

The boy remembered then that it was another of his tasks to pump water. If he forgot to work the rotary pump that pushed water up to the tank in the roof then the Chinaman turned his taps in vain and consequently came out into the yard and beat him, as Fat Uncle sometimes did, with a thin, spearlike length of bamboo.

He was only too well aware of the significance of the hand on the tap and he slipped through the kitchen swiftly and soundlessly, bringing himself up sharply beyond the door that led into the front saloon, where the first figure he saw was that of Edison, who was waving a drumstick, and the first voice he heard was that of the young French doctor:

'I simply ask you this – is the schooner seaworthy? That's all. And you answer me neither one way nor the other.'

With a gesture of expansive sarcasm Edison waved the drumstick.

'Seaworthy? Seaworthy? Of course she's seaworthy. Take a look at her before she falls in half.'

Cane blinds drawn against the heat across the openings beyond the cubicles made the interior of the hotel shadowy and it
was some moments before the boy could make out the figures
of both Edison and the doctor, sitting in one of the cubicles, and
the face of a girl he thought at first was Ginette.

As his eyes became used to the shadows he saw presently
that it was not Ginette. The hair of the girl who sat in the
cubicle was less dense and was plaited. Her body was feline,
compact and rather small and sometimes she sucked at a long
glass, through a straw.

'You don't seem to be able to get it into your head that the
schooner is the only means of communication we've got,' the
young doctor said. His voice was restless with urgency. 'Can't
you see that? Don't you understand?'

'Communication?'

Edison said, 'God, there's bags of communication.' He waved
the drumstick. 'Walk along the water-front. You'll find twenty
canoes. They'll take you.'

'A hundred and thirty miles?' the doctor said. 'It would take
a week. I want someone there tonight. Tomorrow morning
anyway. That's why it's got to be the schooner.'

'Got to be? Got to be? Hark at that,' Edison said. 'Hark at
that.'

There was hardly more than a word or two in this conversation that the boy could fully understand. He watched with
fascination the sarcastic swings of Edison's drumstick and the
upraised restless hands of the doctor, fingers upstretched in
protest or appeal.

'Will you take her?' the young doctor said. 'That's all I'm
asking. Will you take her?'

'Not on your life.'

'I'm not asking you on your life,' the doctor said. 'I'm asking
you on the lives of the people on the island. Perhaps all of you.
God man, in three days we'll have a ramping, raging epidemic
here!'

'Will we?' Edison said. 'If I'm going to snuff it I'll snuff it here in the hotel. In comfort. Not in that bloody colander out there.'

'I don't believe you even half grasp what the situation is,' the doctor said. 'Not a quarter –'

'Hell, it's probably only bellyache.' Edison, picking up a whisky bottle, poured out half a tumbler and pushed the bottle across the table towards the doctor. 'Help yourself. Give 'em all a shot of bug-killer.'

Before the doctor could move or speak again the boy saw Ginette, for the first time, as she moved across the cane blind beyond the cubicle. Half encased in her mass of black hair she had been so much part of the shadow that he had never noticed her there.

Now she simply came forward, halted a foot or two from the table and looked at Edison.

'If you won't take her, Fat Uncle will take her.'

'Fat Uncle. That fat idiot? My God, Fat Uncle?'

'And if Fat Uncle won't take her I'll take her myself.'

'You. Fat Uncle. Fat Uncle. You.'

With contempt Edison threw away the drumstick. It landed among the drums and cymbals on the little dais where Edison and Fat Uncle sat on Saturdays to play for dancing. In the silence that followed Edison drank again. The doctor did not speak and the girl sucked at her straw.

In fascination the boy stood watching Ginette. He saw her put her hands, palms outspread, on the flanks of her big hips. He watched her throw back her head, tossing the thick mass of hair from her shoulders. On her face was a look he had never seen there before. It struck him as being a look of calm, proud loathing.

A moment later she started to move towards the door where the boy stood watching. She still did not speak. As she moved away from the cubicle, Edison, in a further gesture of contempt, put one arm round the waist and under the naked arms of the girl beside him and the girl, in the act of sucking at her glass, laughed suddenly so that she seemed to spit down the straw.

'I'm going to ask Fat Uncle. Even Fat Uncle has grown up from being a sucking-pig.'

The boy saw Edison seize the bottle as if it were a hammer and a moment later he himself was through the kitchen, running, afraid the crash of the bottle would wake the Chinaman, who in turn would start yelling for water. But the crash, for some reason, never came and he was beyond the kitchen and across the yard and inside the shed, waking Fat Uncle, before he recovered from fear and astonishment.

In the shed he had a further moment of astonishment when the girl arrived. In a few seconds it rose to a strange elation. Suddenly, and for the first time, as the girl began to speak to Fat Uncle, now pulling himself lethargically and still only half awake to sit on a soda-water crate, he began to understand what had been going on between Edison, Ginette and the young French doctor in the front part of the hotel.

He surmised, with exultation, that the schooner might, at last, be going to sea. The boat that went like a bird and in which Fat Uncle had splendidly roved the world, in the fashion of a sea-king, was about to sail, miraculously and unbelievably, beyond the reef again.

'There is great danger,' the girl said. 'I mean not with the boat. From the epidemic. We have to be in Papeete tomorrow morning and pick up things for the doctor and then come back quickly. Does the engine work?'

Ape-like and groping, Fat Uncle sat shaking his head.

'It's not my boat. It's Edison's boat.'

'He'll come. He's drunk now. But he'll come.'

'Will the doctor come too?'

'No: the doctor won't come. He'll stay here, with the sick ones. But I'll come.'

It did not seem to the boy that there was either fear or reluctance on the face of Fat Uncle, scratching his head as he pored, eyes groping, over the soda-bottling machine. It was altogether impossible for Fat Uncle, the man of great voyages, the creator of infinite legends, to show fear or reluctance. Fat Uncle was the man who had never been afraid. He interpreted it merely as the uncertainty of a man suddenly waking from sleep and finding himself momentarily stunned by the shattering import of news he had long wanted to hear.

'Does the engine work, I asked you?'

'I can't do it. I could never do it. It's Edison's boat.'

'You've got to do it. The whole island may die if you don't do it. All of us. You too.'

The shattered, crumbling figure of Fat Uncle stood up. The boy looked up at him with sensations of rising exultant pride. He felt too that he suddenly loved the gross, simple, bloated mass of flesh in a way quite unexperienced, quite unknown, before.

'It's Edison's boat. He'll never let me.'

'He'll let you. I'll see to it. He'll let you.'

'And what if he won't? What then?'

'He'll come,' she said. 'You didn't see him when I called him sucking-pig.'

In another moment a sensation of exorbitant impossible hope ran through the boy. In a dazzling second of revelation he realized that he was within reach of becoming one with Fat Uncle, with the girl and perhaps with Edison, on the schooner. He too might be able to go.

'Fat Uncle, Fat Uncle,' he started to say and touched the arm of the quaking mass of flesh still groping about the centre of the hut.

The shock of his touch on the nervous flesh of the man was so great that Fat Uncle swung the elephantine arm that so often hit him when the soda-bottling machine became jammed. But now the arm trembled so much that it did not strike him and a moment later the Chinaman was yelling across the yard:

'No water! No water! I kill you one of these days!'

The voice seemed to give Fat Uncle a remarkable burst of courage. The boy, caught between the stumbling, swearing figure and the menace of the Chinaman in the yard, darted to one side, trying to escape, only to be caught this time by a lumbering backhander that knocked him off his feet.

'Get out of my way!' he shouted. 'I got things to do – I got things on my mind! Can't you see? Things on my mind!'

For the rest of the afternoon the boy pumped water. Sometimes on days when he forgot to fill the tank he heard a distinct sharp snarl of steam as water hit scalding metal on the exposed roof-top, but today he did not listen for the sound. His ears were on the sea.

From time to time the Chinaman, who did not take his pills either, came out of the kitchen to squeak thin admonitions across the yard:

'I keep you pumping till midnight! See! I teach you to forget to pump! Keep you pumping till midnight!'

When darkness fell with sudden swiftness the boy was still pumping. At intervals he paused to listen, looking across the yard with solemn eyes in the direction of the hotel, but there was never a sound that would tell him what was going on there or if anything was going on at all.

Some time later darkness filled him with a new fear: the fear that Edison, the girl and Fat Uncle might have already manned the schooner, crept beyond the lagoon without his knowing it and disappeared. He could not bear this thought. He instinctively stopped pumping and ran out of the yard and across the water-front without stopping to think of the Chinaman or what he would do when he found he was no longer pumping.

To his great surprise and delight the schooner was still moored at the jetty. He ran on and stood at the water-side, looking at her. A great change, he thought, had come over her. Someone had left a lighted hurricane lamp hanging on the side of the deck-house and the light gave to the entire scabby structure of the boat a golden, ethereal glow.

He had never seen her looking like that; it made him catch his breath to see her bathed in light, mysterious and glowing. Across shallow parts of the lagoon beyond her a few men were already fishing, wading waist-deep in water, carrying their flares above their heads, or in canoes that carried flares on poles.

A moment later he actually felt a flame run through his body as he saw Fat Uncle and the girl appear on deck. He wanted to run forward. Fat Uncle had an oil drum in one hand. He swung the drum lightly as he crossed the deck and the boy knew that it was empty.

In his excitement he was ready to run forward to meet them when he heard, from behind him, the sound of other figures crossing the water-front. He instinctively turned and darted away, as he so often did, from the menace of approaching men, hiding himself behind a palm-roofed structure of three sheets of corrugated iron that formed a stall where, in the day time, a woman sold fruit, green coconuts and slices of water-melon.

From there he saw Edison arrive with the young French doctor. It struck him at once that he was a surprisingly sober Edison. He did not shout or stagger. His voice was hardly upraised at all as he called to Fat Uncle.

'Does she go?'

'No.'

'I told you she wouldn't.'

'I'll have another go at her when it's daylight.'

'She'll never go,' Edison said. 'I tell you. She never was any damn good anyway.'

'She'll go like hell when she gets started,' Fat Uncle said.

'When,' Edison said. 'When.'

He approached the gang-plank that connected the schooner with the jetty. He spoke now with compressed sarcasm.

'Another thing you forgot,' he said. 'It costs money to run that thing. Who's paying that?'

The boy saw the girl fling up her head, for the second time that day, with a gesture of proud, sharp loathing.

'So that's what's worrying you,' she said.

'Gas costs money,' Edison said. 'Oil costs money. And it's a damn long way.'

'To where?' she said. 'Hell?'

The boy heard Edison laughing.

'A damn long way in that thing,' he said. 'Well, who pays? I don't pay, I tell you that.'

The young doctor, approaching the gang-plank, spoke for the first time.

'I will pay,' he said, 'or rather the *Institut* will pay. Dr Gregory will see to that.'

'Suits me.'

'Now you have to be shamed into it,' the girl said. 'Now it's money.'

'Don't goad me,' Edison said.

'Goad you? Let your heart goad you,' she said. 'If that's possible.'

'Get off the boat!' Edison started shouting. 'Go on! – the pair of you. Come off her!' His voice started to raise itself, for the first time in cold fury. 'She stays where she is!'

He seemed about to spring forward, as if ready to snatch Fat Uncle and the girl from the deck with his own hands, but the young doctor took several strides forward too.

'It's imperative that she goes,' he said. 'Edison, I tell you it's absolutely imperative that she goes.'

'Goes? I tell you she'll never get beyond the reef –'

'I will buy the boat,' the young doctor said. 'I will give you a cheque on the *Banque D'Indo-China* as a deposit and we will fix the rest when Dr Gregory comes back. How is that? Will you sell her?'

'No.'

'All right. I will hire the boat. I will give you a cheque for that. I will pay for the oil too.' The doctor spoke with succinct, flat contempt, not raising his voice. 'I will also pay Uncle to take her. I am even willing to pay you if it will make you happy.'

'All right!' Edison started shouting. 'All right! So you hired yourself a tea-chest! Now what? All you have to do is pull a string and she's off like a bomb.'

'She'll start.'

'And who's going to start her?' Edison said. He lifted thin, jeering hands in the direction of Fat Uncle. 'That baboon? That bladder? He's been trying all night!'

'I am going to start her.'

'Confident man. Confident man,' Edison said. 'All confidence. She's never been started in six months. Nine months. How do you know she'll start?'

'Because,' the young doctor said. 'I have faith she will start. And because –.' He was already walking towards the plank, rolling up the long white sleeves of his shirt – 'I like talking to engines. They'll start if you talk to them the right way.'

The doctor walked across the plank to the deck of the schooner. Edison retreated a few paces, preparing, it seemed, to go back to the hotel. And then suddenly, as if actually shamed by something the girl had said or as if the thinnest of the doctor's veiled ironies had at last begun to have their effect, he turned and shouted towards the doctor:

'She kicks like hell. She kicks back at you.'

'I'll manage.'

'There's a knack in it. You can stop her kicking if you know the knack.'

'Thanks. I'll manage.'

His voice faded as he disappeared into the well of the boat below the little deck-house. For a few moments longer the hurricane lamp remained suspended where it was. Then Fat Uncle took it off its hook, ready to follow the doctor below, and Edison called:

'Hey, Fat Uncle!'

'Hullo?'

'I'll be back in ten minutes if you want me.'

'Back?'

'We'll need food, won't we, you fat ape?' he called. 'We may be days in that thing. We'll need a case of bug-killer.'

Edison turned abruptly and walked across the water-front. For a moment longer the hurricane lamp illuminated the deck. Then Fat Uncle took it away.

The girl did not move from her position in the stern of the schooner. In darkness broken only by the occasional passage of a fishing flare across the lagoon behind her she leaned on the wooden rail of the boat, staring ashore. Something about her seemed to brood profoundly, in some way mutinously, with sadness, in the darkness.

What it was the boy had no means of knowing. He crouched for a long time behind the water-melon stall. He saw Edison reappear from the hotel, carrying crates and a second hurricane lamp, and then some time later appear a second time, carrying drums of oil.

All this time the girl did not move from the stern of the schooner, but some hours later the boy heard on the night air a new, thrilling and altogether miraculous sound. It made him start to his feet so suddenly that he cracked his elbow on the corrugated iron of the little stall. He was afraid for a moment that someone from the schooner would hear the sound and come down and find him hiding there, afterwards surrendering him to the Chinaman and the tortures of the pump again. But the girl lifted her head no higher than she might have done if she had heard the sound of a rat exploring a tin-can across the jetty.

He listened to the sound of the schooner engine for a long time. When finally it stopped on the night air and Fat Uncle had taken away the second hurricane lamp and there were no more figures on the schooner he felt he could still hear it, wonderfully beating through the darkness. All his blood was on fire with that sound.

Even when he climbed on board and lay down in the hold, in the bows of the boat, in complete darkness, he still imagined he could hear it, a great pulse marvellously driving his blood, miraculously ready to bear him out to sea.

He dozed off and came to himself some hours later, in the first light of morning, in a world of shaking timbers. The reality of the engine actually running in its confined cradle at the foot of the small companionway no longer struck him as beautiful. He felt his blood begin to blench at the smell of engine-oil. His veins felt white and cold. His impression was that they were filled with whiteness.

After he had been sick two or three times, retching as quietly as he could into a sack, he sat up. The boat progressed in a series of deep fat rolls that were so regular that after a time he let his body go with them without any attempt at resistance. Presently, in this way, he beat the last of his sickness.

He was not afraid. He remembered over and over again some words of Fat Uncle's: 'The sea is your friend. There is no need to be afraid of the sea.' At the same time he experienced occasional short moods of disappointment. The boat seemed to progress neither like the wind nor like a bird. It seemed much more like a thick slow slug crawling its way through waters he could not see.

He longed to go on deck. He began to feel, and then to be sure, that the world on deck would be the world he had imagined: his promised world, the world in which the boat flew on a strong white wind, the world of great fish with mouths like doors, the world of Fat Uncle, the King, and the far, long voyages.

The heat of the day was already rising when he dared at last to crawl on deck. Sun struck him brassily as he lifted his face above the companion-way. At this moment, he feared Fat Uncle. He was sure that Fat Uncle would strike him.

Instinctively he searched the deck for Fat Uncle and at first saw only Edison, standing at the wheel, looking ahead, his back towards him. Then he saw Fat Uncle lying flat on his belly, face turned sideways across the deck. It astonished the boy very much to see that his lips were grey.

With wide eyes Fat Uncle lay and stared at him. His mouth fell open. A dribble of yellow moisture poured from his lips. He raised himself on one elbow and with the other hand pawed at his face, gropily, as if pulling at invisible cobwebs.

Then like an enormous frog he inflated his chest and face and let out a gigantic croak that brought Edison whipping round from the wheel. The croak became a thinning whimper. The eyes squeezed themselves shut. They remained shut for the space of a quarter of a minute or so. Then suddenly they shot open again and Fat Uncle, with a yell, told himself of the reality of the boy:

'It is you! It is you! You came up there like a ghost.'

'For Christ sake,' Edison said.

The boy stood at the head of the small companion-way, waiting to be struck. It surprised him greatly that no one moved to strike him. It surprised him still more to see that Fat Uncle, the man of the sea, lifting himself to his knees, face grey and sickened, looked as frightened as he felt himself.

'How in hell did you get here?' Edison said.

He started trembling and had nothing to answer. His veins ran white again. The sea ran white about the schooner. He felt sick again as he stared at its running whiteness and the faces of the men.

In a third great moment of surprise he saw the girl walking up from the stern of the schooner. He had never remotely expected to see her there. He had expected the world of men to be completed, for some reason, by the young French doctor.

Fat Uncle, as the girl appeared, experienced one of his sudden waves of courage and waved an elephantine fist at the boy. He lurched unsteadily as he threw the blow with vague menace, like a drunk, but the blow missed by a yard.

'That's right. Strike him,' the girl said. 'Be brave. Strike him.'

'I ought to throw the little squirt overboard!' Edison said. 'Shark-wards.'

'That's it. You be brave too,' she said.

It was Edison now who started yelling. He yelled for Fat Uncle to take the wheel. Then he grabbed the boy by the shirt and yelled into his face:

'How the hell did you creep in?' With an open hand he cuffed him first on one side of his face, then the other. He bawled incomprehensibly, narrow face raging. Then he turned on Fat Uncle, yelling: 'You were supposed to keep him working, you fat baboon, out back there. What in hell were you up to?'

After this, since there was no answer from Fat Uncle, he cuffed the boy about the face again, knocking him from side to side.

'You are very brave, too,' the girl said.

'Shut up and lie down somewhere !' Edison yelled.

'You didn't used to talk to me like that,' she said.

'I talk how I like.'

'Everybody knows.'

'And another thing – I'm in charge here,' Edison yelled. 'I'm skipper. This is my boat.'

'Come with me. Come this way,' the girl said and held out her hand to the boy.

The boy followed her to the stern end of the deck. She was preparing food there: bread, with a little rice and scrapings of raw fish and a few red peppers. A half stalk of bananas lay on the deck, together with Edison's crate of whisky.

'Why did you come?' she said.

He did not know why he had come. He stared at the sea's running whiteness. A snowy wake between himself and a jagged glitter of horizon held him transfixed. He discovered that he could no longer tell why he had come, why he wanted to come or of the great thoughts that had once pounded through him. Most of all the great thoughts had vanished, meaningless or incomprehensible, and would not come back.

'There's no need to be afraid of anything,' she said. 'Don't be afraid.'

'Why did you come?' he said.

She did not answer. She turned her head away, face half-hidden by the huge black mass of her hair. She sat cross-legged as she busied herself with the fish, her big legs and feet bare, her knees golden and shining, her *pereu* drawn up above them. Her hair, when it fell the full length and she was sitting down, as she was now, was thick and long enough to spread about her like a cloak.

'Why did you come?' he said. 'I didn't think you were coming.'

'I came like you did,' she said. 'Hiding.'

He sat cross-legged too, staring at her. He remembered how she had leaned against the stern of the schooner, in complete darkness, brooding. Was it possible that she brooded about coming? He watched the whiteness of the sea, the hot, glittering light, running past her dark head. Her splendid, gentle, brooding face was carved against the skyline that ran in the heat of the morning like pure flame.

He started wondering, for some reason, how old she was. She looked, he thought, much older than yesterday: much older than the day he had heard her laughing so loudly in the presence of the two doctors. He could not remember seeing her laugh ever since that time.

He guessed that she would be old. Everybody who was grown-up was old. That was natural. It was only people like himself who were not old and he said now, solemnly:

'How old are you? I never knew how old you were.'

She actually laughed a little, showing her broad white teeth.

'As old as my tongue and a little older than my teeth,' she said.

'So am I.'

'Sixteen,' she said. 'That's how old I am.'

'Is that old?' he said.

'I sometimes think,' she said, 'it's as old as I ever want to be.'

They went on talking together, sometimes busy with the food, sometimes doing nothing, for most of the morning. The swell across the ocean seemed to lengthen with the heat of the day. The candescent wake of the slugging schooner grew no faster but simply whitened more fiercely, blinding in the perpendicular sun.

Towards twelve o'clock Edison came aft for a few minutes, picked a whisky bottle out of the crate and stood with it in his hand, drinking, staring out to sea. The girl did not speak to him. Edison did not speak to either. A two-day growth of beard seemed to make the long lean face appear more cadaverous in the fierce upward reflection of sea-light. Sweat gave it a thin oily gleam, the naked ball-like head quite shadowlesss in the ferociously burning glow of noon.

He spoke only once, and then not to the girl. Walking away, pausing half a dozen paces up the deck, he waved the bottle in a starboard direction, out to an ocean apparently empty except for a distant, long-winged sea-bird flying low above the water.

'Look, boy. See that?'

The boy looked up in time to see, fifty yards away, the explosion of a single rising shark. It sprang from the water like a suddenly discharged torpedo and then vanished instantly, seeming to leave on the hot air an echo that in reality was Edison's voice, laughing.

'See you behave, boy,' Edison said, 'or that's where you go.'

He swung away towards the wheel, lifting the bottle to his mouth, indulging his favourite habit of drinking as he walked. From the wheel the boy heard him laugh again, as if perhaps he were repeating the joke to Fat Uncle, who in turn laughed too.

After that the boy sat for some long time quite silent. It was beyond him to know if the threat of Edison were real or if the laughter of Edison was only laughter. He was aware, in a strange way, of a growing expansion of the sea about him. Noon now seemed to impose on it a sombre, heartless enormity. The shark that had sprung suddenly out of the heart of it was an evil vision that was also a threatening voice. The recollection of its moment of furious savagery made him shudder.

There was no way he knew of expressing himself about these things and he simply sat staring at the gentle, brooding face of the girl.

'When will we arrive?' he said. 'Today?'

'Perhaps tonight. If all goes well.'

He wanted very much to arrive. The air was growing thicker and more oppressive every moment and he was glad to see the girl pouring out, into an enamel cup, a drink of water.

Drinking the water, he sat staring, in his long-sighted, solemn fashion, far out to sea. It had occurred to him suddenly that he might see land there. By searching for land he might project himself into a still further world, beyond Edison's sinister jocularities and the voice of the shark, where no one could threaten him any more.

For the space of a few seconds he actually believed he could see land, in a purplish, uncertain mass, looming from the horizon. He watched this mass for some moments longer without certainty. Then it began to seem to him nebulously, ominously, unlike land.

He spoke to the girl, pointing.

'Is that where we're going?' he said. 'Is that the land?'

The girl rose on her knees in order to look more easily over the side of the schooner. In this alert, upright posture she let out a sudden gasp of alarm. A moment later she had twisted herself completely to her feet and was running along the deck.

'Look there! Look there!' she was shouting. 'That way! Look there!'

The boy stood motionless, watching the horizon with its ominous flower of darkening cloud, and knew suddenly that it was not the land.

He lay below in the hold, side by side with the girl, in complete darkness, when the storm hit them from the south.

All morning he had been aware of a wind of splendid whiteness on the sea. Now he knew that what hit them was a black wind. It was a wind of solid, driving water. He felt it pounding against the wooden bows of the schooner in an unbroken attack that sent him rolling like a light and helpless barrel across the timbers and then pushed him back again. He yelled in pain as his head cracked on the bulwark and for the first time in his life he could hear no responsive sound of his own voice against the roar of wind and rain.

Somewhere in the middle of this maelstrom of driving sound an object crashed with sickening thunder down the steps of the companion-way. The boy did not know until afterwards that this was Fat Uncle. With a tremendous clang that seemed for a moment like the side of the ship exploding inwardly, the hatch-cover closed behind him, battening three of them down.

It was impossible for him to know how long the black wind beat at them. The squat flatness of the boat kept her riding down long troughs that, just as she seemed to be free, curled like vast conical hooks and clawed her back again. At each end of these raging troughs she was so low in the water, leaking at the seams, that he lay half-drowned.

When the wind began to lessen with a sinister abruptness that startled him far more than his first sight of the storm-cloud had done, he became gradually aware of an ominous situation. He could not hear the engine beating. All he could hear above the dying wind were the elephantine hands of Fat Uncle, clawing their way, ape-like, up the totally dark steps of the hatchway.

An astonishing shaft of metallic sunlight seemed to dart down through the opening hatch and scooped Fat Uncle up to the deck. The boy heard Edison yelling. In a sudden list of the schooner water from the deck poured down the steps and it was as if Fat Uncle had turned and spewed.

Edison yelled again. In stumbling response Fat Uncle re-appeared at the top of the hatchway and a moment later slithered down it. He began to make frantic and misdirected attacks on the engine, banging pointlessly with spanners. Water sloshed about the hold, drenching the boy as it climbed up the bulwarks and bounced back again.

He stared at the fumbling figure of Fat Uncle with a mixture of brooding hope and pity. The huge hands, convulsively picking up tools and groping about the engine cradle, were pathetic in their obstinate impression of doing something useful. Now and then they hovered, jelly-like, above the puzzle of plugs and mechanism, fingering objects with timidity, as if they were monsters that would sting.

Suddenly an enraged, half-drunk Edison threw himself down the hatchway. He yelled incomprehensible threats at Fat Uncle and struck him flat-handed about the face. The great yellow ape dived sideways as the boy so often dived in retreat from him and then fell, deflated, into the sloppy water of the hold.

'Get up on deck, you fat bastard!' Edison yelled. 'Get hold of the wheel and try to keep her steady when she goes!'

Watching the drenched and yellow figure heaving itself up the hatchway the boy suddenly felt infinitely sorry for Fat

Uncle. A moment later he saw Edison pounding the gross flopping back with his knee.

'Get up there! Go on, you bastard! Out of the way – I want to get on deck. Move yourself! – God, you got us into this thing, didn't you, but you've got about as much bloody idea how to get us out as a sea-egg.'

The two men disappeared on deck. A rush of wind blew away the last of Edison's disturbed threats. A minute later it seemed to blow the man himself back again. He had armed himself with two bottles. He was actually performing, as he came down the hatchway, his trick of drinking as he walked.

He too made attacks on the engine. A thin enraged strength gave the white unmuscular arms a wiry, clockwork activity. It was unbrutal but sinister. At intervals he slapped his mouth against the bottle. With the return of sunlight the air had become cinderous again and presently Edison ripped off his shirt. The prominent white ribs, curiously hairless, were bathed in sweat, and the boy suddenly saw him as a living, clawing, mechanical skeleton.

An hour later the engine was still not working and periodically Edison stormed at it with disjointed shouts. In a lurch of the boat an oil drum freed itself from somewhere and rolled against his shins, setting him yelling in a venomous tirade against Fat Uncle, the French doctor and above all the monstrous stupidity of ever having come on the boat. Fat Uncle was mad. The boat was a death-trap. Longuemart was mad. Who ever had the damn crazy idea of taking her out in the first place?

'You did, you fat bastard, didn't you? You did!'

Time measured itself in the emptying of a bottle. He uncorked another. As the level of this second one lowered itself the skeleton-like figure of Edison seemed to disappear. A trapped, blasphemous prisoner took its place: a prisoner of an engine that would not work and of a vision so disturbed that he actually started to aim misplaced blows at the bulwarks as if hammering to be free.

In a final abusing storm of threats he lurched wildly up the companionway, swinging the spanner. The boy heard him scream hoarsely on a harsh upward scale of abuse, incoherent to him except in a final repeated phrase:

'I'm coming for you, you fat bastard! I'm coming for you!'

At the moment of Edison's disappearance the boy saw the girl emerge from the darkness behind the engine cradle. Her *pereu*, like her arms and legs, was drenched in oil and water.

She picked up a hammer left by Edison on the engine cover. She stood for a moment at the foot of the steps. The boy scrambled across the partly flooded hold, stumbling in water. She seemed to take pity on the anxious brooding eyes and put one hand on his shoulder.

He heard running feet on the deck.

'Stay here,' she said. 'Don't come up. Keep away.'

She started up the steps. A gust of wind shuddering down the companionway blew away the complete coherence of whatever she said next but he thought it sounded like:

'He gets filled with madness. The whisky blinds him. He doesn't see –'

In three or four leaps she was up the steps. Sheer curiosity could not keep him back and less than half a minute later he was crawling after her.

He emerged on to what seemed to him a steaming, deserted deck. Heat was burning up the last of the flood of spray and rain. The deck planks were giving off grey rising vapour.

He found himself suspended in fear and excitement at the head of the companionway. His hands and knees felt locked. When he did move at last it was to retreat a step or two as Edison tore blindly past him, yelling, with Fat Uncle a yard or two ahead.

He heard Fat Uncle fall, screaming, against the wheel. He knelt cold and transfixed as Edison beat at the yellow mass of flesh with the spanner.

The girl came running too. She aimed a single blow at Edison's shoulder with the hammer. A second before the impact Edison turned his head sharply as if to shout to her to keep away and the blow crushed into the smooth white top of the balding skull.

Edison fell sightlessly. A moment of awful surprise seemed to click his mouth open. A gust of sea-wind seemed to blow a thin feather of blood from his lips. A second gust of wind caught the entire body as it fell, pitching it suddenly, frail and more than ever skeleton-like, against the wheel, where Fat Uncle lay.

The boy stood for what seemed to him a long time surveying the dead. It would not have surprised him very much if the girl had been dead too. She sat stiffly against the side of the deck, head bowed, face completely hidden in the mass of her hair.

He was disturbed at last by a vague notion that the dead ought to be covered. He walked back towards the stern of the schooner and presently found a tarpaulin in a locker. He dragged it back along the deck, spread it out and threw it at last over the bodies of Edison and Fat Uncle.

Turning away, he felt his veins run white again. The wind was white on the water. The heat of the afternoon was incredibly, cruelly white as it beat up from the drying decks and the sea.

He turned at last to the girl. With relief he saw her lift her face, as if she had actually been watching him from the cavernous shadow of her hair. The most mysterious thing about her face, he thought, was that she seemed now to be in one respect like Edison. She could not see.

He was prepared for her to start screaming. She did not scream. Instead she turned her face slowly in the direction of the wheel and held it there, transfixed by the sight of the tarpaulin.

He also stared at the tarpaulin. The flaring realization that it covered the body of the man of legends, the great, long voyager, filled him with sudden waves of sorrow for Fat Uncle.

He turned and saw this sorrow of his reflected in her face. Somehow he grasped, incredibly, that it might be sorrow for Edison. He could not understand this. He could remember nothing good of Edison. His abiding impressions of Edison were of a man repellent, sneering, drunken, wasteful, odiously sinister. Edison was of the breed for whom he played on Saturday evenings at the screaming dances: a dirty man.

It even occurred to him, as he stood there for a few moments longer, that sorrow for Edison was a mistaken thing. It even seemed to him possible to be glad that Edison was dead. He even thought the girl might be glad.

When he spoke for the first time it was with an odd detachment, about something he felt to be far removed from these realities.

'That was a great storm,' he said. 'I've never known a storm like that.'

'No,' she said. 'It was a great storm.'

As she spoke she turned to look at him, for the first time directly, with large black eyes. A sudden burst of wind blew her hair free of her face, leaving it fully exposed. Its sightless lack of expression seemed to imprison her in a terrible bond.

In this same imprisoned, expressionless way she spoke monotonously of the engine:

'Does the engine work?' she said. 'What about the engine?'

He was glad to follow her down the steps of the companionway. In the hold it was easier, now more secure; the sea was calming down. In the partial gloom he could not see her face so well and he was glad of this. He was glad too to be out of sight of the humped black mound that was Fat Uncle and Edison.

'When did you hide?' she said.

'In the morning. Early. After everyone had gone.'

'I think I was asleep when you came,' she said. 'Do you remember they went back to the hotel and then came back again? That was when I hid. I heard the doctor working on the engine for an hour.'

As she spoke she seemed to be searching for something and a second later he knew what it was.

'We must have the spanner,' she said.

With nausea and fear he remembered where the spanner

was. As she realized it too she stood imprisoned more terribly than ever, unable to move or speak to him.

He went up the companionway. Once more, on deck, his veins ran with whiteness. The sea, running with whiteness too, blazed at his eyeballs.

For a few seconds longer, standing over the tarpaulin, he played a game of hideous guess-work. He guessed that the larger, humpier mound underneath the tarpaulin was the body of Fat Uncle. He guessed that Edison had the spanner.

He snatched at the tarpaulin with sudden desperation and the empty hands of Edison were revealed underneath it. He flung it back again and turned to find himself mocked in the glitter of whiteness prancing up from the sea.

The spanner lay all the time on the deck, six feet away.

'Here it is,' he said to her.

It was the instinctive thing to give her the spanner as he reached the foot of the hatchway and she promptly dropped it.

He picked it up. Something about the feel of the spanner made him suddenly recall Fat Uncle. He was abruptly glad of Fat Uncle. Sometimes when the soda-bottling machine jammed it was a favourite theme of Fat Uncle's to bludgeon him into the business of mending it again. His hands, in consequence, had grown quite agile with spanners.

He began to tinker with the engine. The girl brooded beside him, sombrely, terribly quiet. By contrast he began to feel less and less of his nausea, his fear and his horror at the bloody secrets of the tarpaulin up on deck. The spanner gave him the means of grasping at tangible things and he began now to try to cheer the girl up with recollections:

'Fat Uncle went on long voyages in this boat,' he said. 'Once he was blown by a big wind like that.'

'Yes?'

'To Australia. All the way to Australia the wind blew him.'

'I never heard him talk of that.'

'A million miles,' he said.

'There is no such thing as a million miles.'

'There must be,' he said. 'Fat Uncle told me so.'

He felt himself become buoyant at these recollections.

'Long, long voyages he went. To Noumea. Across the world. Everywhere.'

'Long ago?'

'Oh ! long ago.'

'I never heard him talk of it.'

Two hours later he could no longer see to work on the engine. In his own mind he had long since given up the idea that anything he could do would make it work again. His pretence of solving its mysteries was merely part of his pride.

He followed the girl up the hatchway. With averted eyes the pair of them went aft along the deck.

'There is a little food left,' she said, 'if you feel like it.'

He could only shake his head. A spurt of sickness squeezed itself acidly up his throat. He managed to say:

'Do you feel like it?'

'Some water, perhaps. Could you drink some water?'

He could not speak this time. He simply nodded his head.

'The sun has gone,' she said.

Holding the water cask in readiness to fill the mug with water, she paused and stood for some time staring at the horizon. The sun had gone down in a startling agony of carmine, purple-black and flame. A few pinkish clouds, like high birds, were flying far overhead, delicate, broken-feathered. The sea, calm now except for the faintest ripples, collected these colours and cast the mingled glow of them back in her face. The features of the face were set and grim, as if carved, their proudness undissolved.

Ten minutes later it was utterly dark except for a slowly expiring gap of rosy copper low down and far away, against the face of the dead calm sea. Something about this calmness, on which the schooner now rode as if locked to an invisible anchor, filled the air with a sense of foreboding so ominous that when the boy finally lay down on the deck, side by side with the girl, it was with his face downwards but slightly averted, listening.

It struck him suddenly that they were there for ever. The schooner was locked against a sea permanently held in deathly

silence. Its searing flare of daylight whiteness had given place
to a darkness that imprisoned every scrap of motion. He could
not detect the slightest drift of the boat one way or another or
the faintest rise of it up and down.

He lay there for a long time in this motionless attitude, completely locked in silence. The girl too was lying face downwards,
head buried in her hair. Her hands in turn clutched the side of
her hair, as if in a nightmare of remorse and terror she was
suspended in the act of tearing it out by the roots.

The horror of what she must be thinking broke on him very
gradually. After a long time he turned and lay face upwards,
staring at the stars. The sky, like the sea, seemed to be held in
a formidable, dark paralysis.

Staring upward, he wondered what he himself could possibly
feel like if he had killed a man. Through a horror of his own
he passed into a stage of sheer fright at the mere recollection of
what lay under the tarpaulin along the deck. When the horror
finally lessened and passed it gave way to an enormous sense of
wonder: a thankful wonder that he had not, after all, killed a
man, and then a terrible wonder that he had actually seen the
act, survived it and was alive to remember it all.

He lay for a little longer in a senseless vacuum, no longer
even thinking. A dozen times before this he had expected her
to cry. The fact that she did not once show the faintest sign of
tears had helped to keep him from weeping too. Suddenly he
could not bear any longer her tearless agonized attitude of seeming to tear her hair out by the roots as she lay there in the darkness. It filled him with a boyish rush of compassion in which he
could no longer refrain from touching her. He moved towards
her and put his hands on her shoulders and her hair.

She at once interpreted this groping touch of his as a sign of
fear. She turned instinctively and with big naked arms held
him against her. She rocked him backwards and forwards,
mother-wise, murmuring quietly at the same time.

He found something more than comfort in the touch of her
body. It did for him what the sky and the sea had failed to do.
It drove away the last impression of ominous foreboding, his

feeling that the two of them were locked there for ever. It coaxed him out of his senseless vacuum.

The girl too began to come alive. She actually pressed her mouth against the side of his face. Then he heard her voice framing words for the first time since darkness had come down.

'Don't be afraid.'

'I'm not afraid.' As he said this she enveloped him still more closely with her body. 'Are you afraid?'

'It is not a question of being afraid.'

He did not understand this remark and for some moments she did not explain it. Instead she held him still more closely to her, arms completely round him now.

'There is something more than being afraid.'

For a second time he did not understand her. He was bewildered by a growing sense of mystery about her. Her flesh quivered as she held him. An impression that all the pores of her skin were about to shed their own terrible fears gave him an overwhelming sense of sorrow that he could not bear.

'What is it?' he said. 'What is more than being afraid?'

She spoke with distant calmness in answer.

'I have a child inside me.'

He did not speak. The gravity of his pride that she had decided to tell him this was so great that he felt suddenly, inside himself, a new stature. He was also old. He also felt he had become, in some strange way, part of her.

'Shall we try to sleep now?' she said.

Her voice had taken on a further spell of calmness. The infinite sense of brooding sorrow was at last dispelled.

'Come closer to me,' she said. 'Lie close to me.'

He had already closed his eyes. He started, a little later, to sleep peacefully in the warmth of her arms. In the uncanny silence of the completely motionless boat she slept too, holding him like a mother.

He awoke, some time after dawn, to strange noises. He thought at first that the sea had risen and was beating against the sides of the vessel. He opened his eyes and stared upward at a repetition of the flocks of clouds travelling, like pink birds, high across the morning sky.

The sounds troubled him. Like part of a half-remembered dream they mocked at his expanding consciousness with strange familiarity.

Finally he got up. He could no longer resist the reality of the sounds. He walked along the deck. Half way to the bows he stopped, horrified by the astounding emptiness of the deck about the wheel, stunned by an incredible illusion that the tarpaulin had been carefully folded up and laid at the head of the hatchway.

In the moment of realizing that the bodies of Edison and Fat Uncle no longer lay there he realized also that the engine was running.

He stood staring down the steps of the hatchway for fully a minute before realizing that the blood-stained face of the man bending over the engine was the face of Fat Uncle.

A new horror rose up in him. The impression that he was staring down at a figure spirited back from the dead was too much for his calmness. He felt his veins run sick and white again.

Almost at the same moment he heard Fat Uncle begin speaking.

'I remembered we only put half a tank in,' he said. The half-idiotic lips gaped upward, brown with blood. 'No wonder we stopped.'

The boy started to answer with a series of broken phrases that made no sense with the exception of the word 'Edison? Edison?' which he blubbered over and over again.

With fat crooked fingers Fat Uncle waved upwards, towards the rising light.

'He's gone where he said he'd send you,' he said. 'Out there.'

For the first time the boy broke into weeping. His choking tears had nothing to do with Edison, nor with the sudden appearance of Fat Uncle, back from the dead. He was weeping at an unknown horror that seemed to be crawling up from the whitening sea, on all sides of him, in a nightmare.

The sound of his weeping brought the girl running along the deck. She too heard the sound of the engine and stopped abruptly.

'Timi! Timi!' she was shouting. 'Timi!' The sudden joy on her face woke in him fresh bursts of weeping. 'Why do you cry? How did you make it go?'

The head of Fat Uncle rose above the top of the hatchway. And the girl, seeing it, let out her own grievous cry.

A land rose from the sea. A long serrated cockscomb of green and violet seemed to float out of the horizon under a scalding sun.

Like a caricature of a warrior scarred in battle, Fat Uncle stood grasping the wheel with enormous, aggressive hands, staring straight ahead. His face, with muscles set, no longer seemed flabby. It seemed to be contained in a metallic, greasy mask. Dark crusts of blood had congealed and dried across the forehead, heightening the yellow of the skin and giving the impression of a man wrapped in a brooding, savage frown.

The girl once dipped a bucket into the sea. She was moved to bathe the bloodstained face and started to tear a strip of cloth from her *pereu*; but Fat Uncle bashed into the silence of the deck with a slam of a vast hand against the wheel and a bruising cry across the white calm sea.

'Let them stop there! Let the world see them! Let them see how he tried to kill me!'

After that the girl crouched against the side of the boat, head enclosed in the falling mass of her hair, hands flat on the rail. She stared for some hours in speechless concentration at the land enlarging with incredible slowness on the horizon while the boy, ordered by Fat Uncle, washed blood from the deck.

Now and then Fat Uncle broke into long, senseless abuse of Edison. He shouted with lunatic contempt at the evil of fate, spitting at the sea. At the end of these outbursts he struck at the wheel again with a strange mixture of pride and childishness, laughing, giggling fatly.

'Now she's mine! Now I've got her back!' His idiot pride in the material possession of the boat made him seem more than ever swollen. 'She was always mine! She always belonged to me.'

The boy was struck by these outbursts into a watchful awe. He tried for a long time to work out a reason for Fat Uncle's pride in his scars. He understood the pride in the schooner, but that of the scars eluded him completely until Fat Uncle yelled:

'You saw the fight. How did I kill him? Tell me that.'

It did not occur to the boy that this was evidence of cowardice in Fat Uncle. He heard the words with amazed bewilderment. He heard Fat Uncle give a laugh of triumph, as if actually glad that he had killed a man.

He was about to shatter this illusion by telling Fat Uncle the truth when he saw the girl, moving for the first time for some hours, slowly turn her face, pushing back her hair with both hands. The face, paralysed with fright, looked unbelievably cold in the heat of the day, frozen against the background of an ocean across which, at last, a wind was rising, cutting brief slits of foam from the crests of the long smooth swells.

'Tell me how I killed him! I don't remember.' Fat Uncle struck attitudes of boldness, flinging out oil-stained contemptuous arms. 'I remember he came up behind me – like that' – he crouched with grotesque ape-like fury in imitation of Edison – 'Like that he came up, didn't he? I remember that.' He spat again with galling, contemptuous laughter. 'From behind! Like a rat – from behind!'

For a long time the boy nursed his dilemma, watching first the girl, then the land becoming more and more clearly defined every moment across the white-fringed sea. He could actually make out now the collar of the island's enclosing reef and soon he could see the colour of the mountains beyond, yellow-brown at the foot, sharp emerald high up the slopes, with dark palm tufts on the shore and in between.

Once or twice he opened his mouth to speak, but the words never framed themselves. Hearing Fat Uncle laugh again, he pondered gravely, with eyes that seemed as always to be listening to half-formed sounds, on the astonishing fact that a man might be glad to kill a man. Held in a horror between truth and silence, he was troubled by a growing recollection, more bewildering to him now than when it had happened, of the girl telling him of the child inside herself and of her mystifying words:

'There is something more than being afraid.'

These were all strange mysteries, not of his making. He could not interpret them. He could only interpret the embalming warmth of the girl's arms in the depth of night-time, quietening him to sleep, holding him so closely that he was almost one with the other body inside her own.

That was a still stranger mystery: the child inside herself. He brooded on that until compassion and wonder held him in a trance, sightlessly.

He was woken out of it by a yell from Fat Uncle:

'I see the gap!' With the quaking, triumphant fingers of a man who might have made, single-handed, an uncharted voyage across cruel waters, he pointed ahead. 'We're nearly there! Boy, take the wheel a moment while I get below!'

The boy grasped the wheel. In the few seconds while Fat Uncle was below the girl came and stood beside him. He turned, not speaking, and looked at her sad, gentle, brooding face, wrapped in dignity. He searched it for a sign of fear and at the same moment searched his own mind for something to say to her.

A second later the engine slowed to half-speed. She smiled gravely. Without a word she put her hand on his shoulder and a moment later Fat Uncle came up on deck.

'I'll take her now.' He brandished, in his ape-like, childish fashion, a pair of arms that seemed as if they were about to embrace himself. 'I'll take her in.'

As he moved to grasp the wheel the girl spoke quietly.

'Let the boy take her a little farther,' she said. 'He deserves that. It would make him very proud to take her a little farther.'

There were still a few hundred yards to go.

'Take her!' Fat Uncle again waved generous, expansive arms, laughing. 'How does she feel? How do you like her?'

As the boy, grasping the wheel, stared into hot sunlight with solemn far-seeing eyes, a strange illusion affected him. It was that the boat, though down to half-speed, was travelling faster than ever, running with flying swiftness across white-flecked water towards the steaming gap and the mountains beyond.

'How does she feel?' Fat Uncle shouted. 'How does she go?'

The veins of the boy ran with pride. The entire sea about him ran with wonderful whiteness. He turned swiftly to show his pride to the girl and saw that there were tears in her eyes. These tears, unfallen, imprisoned her brooding eyes with a troubled, crystalline brightness. She too was proud.

Exultantly he half-threw up his hands. A boy might travel a million miles and never see what he had seen. He might live through a million nights and never hear what he had heard. Solemnly he was glad he had been afraid with her and because of it he felt he understood, at last, her tears, her pride and above all her brooding darkness.

'She goes like the wind!' he shouted. 'Like the wind!'

More about Penguins

Penguinews, which appears every month, contains details of all the new books issued by Penguins as they are published. From time to time it is supplemented by *Penguins in Print*, which is a complete list of all available books published by Penguins. (There are well over three thousand of these.)

A specimen copy of *Penguinews* will be sent to you free on request, and you can become a subscriber for the price of the postage. For a year's issues (including the complete lists) please send 30p if you live in the United Kingdom, or 60p if you live elsewhere. Just write to Dept EP, Penguin Books Ltd, Harmondsworth, Middlesex, enclosing a cheque or postal order, and your name will be added to the mailing list.

Note: *Penguinews* and *Penguins in Print* are not available in the U.S.A. or Canada

J. A. Baker

The Peregrine

Winner of the Duff Cooper Award

Not since *Cider with Rosie* has any writer celebrated the English countryside with the kind of poetry that John Baker lends to this inspired study of one of the rarest and most beautiful birds of prey.

'It is a masterpiece and instantly takes its place among the great triumphal affirmations of man's search for his lost place in the Universe' – Kenneth Allsop.

'His phrases have a magnesium-flare intensity'
– Christopher Wordsworth.

'A very remarkable book to buy and keep for there will certainly not be another like it' – Brian Vesey-Fitzgerald.

Not for sale in the U.S.A.

H. E. Bates

The Distant Horns of Summer

James's new nanny was seventeen years old and almost as innocent as he was. Life was good together. She entered into his imaginary world. She made friends with his invisible 'mates', Mr Pimm and Mr Monday. Then Mr Ainsworth came along. From the very beginning James's new nanny gave more attention to him. She even played silly games with him . . . like taking off their clothes together. It was enough to make a boy leave home . . .

A Moment in Time

'There would have to be
a war in a summer like this'

She was still in her teens when they came to fight a war in the air. Day by precarious day, she shared with these dedicated youngsters – hardly more than boys – dangers unbearably heightened by the peace of the English countryside.

Not for sale in the U.S.A.

H. E. Bates

Fair Stood the Wind for France

'Perhaps the finest novel of the war ... The scenes are exquisitely done and the characters – tenderly and beautifully drawn – are an epitome of all that is best in the youth of the two countries. This is a fine, lovely book which makes the heart beat with pride' – *Daily Telegraph.*

The Wedding Party

A collection of thirteen short stories ranging from the humour of *The Picnic* and *Early One Morning* to the tragedy of *The Primrose Place* and the drama of sorrow and beauty of *The Wedding Party.*

Also Available

DULCIMA

THE DARLING BUDS OF MAY

A BREATH OF FRENCH AIR

WHEN THE GREEN WOODS LAUGH

OH! TO BE IN ENGLAND*

THE WILD CHERRY TREE

Not for sale in the U.S.A.

* *Not for sale in the U.S.A. or Canada*

H. E. Bates's Best-selling 'Larkin' Books

The Darling Buds of May

Introducing the Larkins, a family with a place in popular mythology.
Here they come, in the first of their hilarious rural adventures, crashing their way through the English countryside in the wake of Pa, the quick-eyed golden-hearted junk-dealer, and Ma, with a mouthful of crisps and a laugh like a jelly.

A Breath of French Air

They're here again – the indestructible Larkins; this time, with Baby Oscar, the Rolls, and Ma's unmarried passport, they're off to France. And with H. E. Bates, you may be sure, there's no French without tears of laughter.

When the Green Woods Laugh

In the third of the Larkin novels H. E. Bates makes the Dragon's Blood and the double scotches hit with no less impact than they did in *The Darling Buds of May* For the full Larkin orchestra is back on the rural fiddle, and (with Angela Snow around) the Brigadier may be too old to ride but he's young enough to fall. 'Pa is as sexy, genial, generous, and boozy as ever. Ma is a worthy match for him in all these qualities' – *The Times*

Oh! to be in England*

Are you taking life too seriously?
What you need is a dose of *Oh! To Be in England* – another splendid thighs-breasts-and-buttercups frolic through the Merrie England of the sixties with the thirsty, happy, lusty, quite uninhibited and now rightly famous junk-dealing family of Larkins.

Not for sale in the U.S.A.

* Not for sale in he U.S.A. or Canada